bobmarley

THE STORIES BEHIND EVERY SONG
1962–1981

Soul Rebel

Author's Dedication
Dedicated to my two beautiful
daughters, Angelique and Natascha... and
to Big Boy and Charlie

THIS IS A CARLTON BOOK

Published in the United States by
THUNDER'S MOUTH PRESS
841 Broadway, Fourth Floor, New York,
NY 10003

Text copyright © Maureen Sheridan
1999
Design copyright © Carlton Books
Limited 1999

Library of Congress Catalog Card
Number 99-60903

ISBN 1 56025 204 9

Distributed by Publishers Group West,
1700 Fourth Street, Berkeley, CA 94710

Printed and bound in Italy

Project Editor: Lucian Randall
Editor: Mick Meikleham
Art Editors: Adam Wright, Phil Scott
Design: Joyce Mason
Picture Research: Catherine Costelloe
Production: Alexia Turner

10 9 8 7 6 5 4 3 2 1

bobmarley

THE STORIES BEHIND EVERY SONG
1962–1981

Soul Rebel

THUNDER'S
MOUTH
PRESS

PICTURE CREDITS

The publishers would like to thank the following sources for their kind permission to reproduce the pictures in this book:

Bridgeman Art Library, London/British Library, London, UK *A true and perfect relation of that..terrible Earthquake at Port Royal in Jamaica, which happened on the 7th June, 1962* 102b/Library of Congress, Washington D.C., USA *The Escaped Slave in the Union Army, from 'Harper's Weekly', 1864 (engraving) (b&w photo) by American Scholol (19th century)* 127
Corbis/Bettmann 83, 99, 106, 111, 120, 126/Bettmann/UPI 96/Bojan Breolj 72/David Cumming/Eye Ubiquitous 68/Howard Davies 6-7/Lyn Goldsmith 53, 101, 115/Daniel Laine 13, 94, 123/Tim Page 87/Neal Preston 46, 116-7/UPI 12
Hulton Getty 104
London Features International Ltd. 34, 39, 54, 56, 80-1/Paul Cox 43/Mick Prior 33
Panos Pictures/Marc French 124
Pictorial Press Ltd. 92-3/Van Houten 71
Redferns/Paul Bergen 90/Ian Dickson 2-3c, 55/Dave Ellis 48-9/John Kirk 23/Keith Morris 134/Michael Ochs Archives 10, 27, 32/David Redfern 17/Ebet Roberts 42, 121, 130/Gai Terrell 136/Charlyn Zlotnik 77
Retna Pictures Ltd./Adrian Boot 20, 103/Chris Craske 128/David Corio 3r, 78, 118/Jill Furmanovsky 60, 110/Gary Gershoff 58/Youri Lenquette 24, 74-5/Michael Putland 40, 50, 84
Dave Saunders 64, 66-7, 108
Maureen Sheridan 37
Peter Simon Photography 6, 8, 14, 18/9, 22, 26, 29, 38, 47, 59, 63, 79, 86, 88, 100, 102t, 112, 122, 137
Topham Picturepoint 2l, 30
Vin Mag Archive Ltd. 133

Every effort has been made to acknowledge correctly and contact the source and/copyright holder of each picture, and Carlton Books Limited apologises for any unintentional errors or omissions which will be corrected in future editions of this book.

CONTENTS

BEGINNINGS

BOB MARLEY (AGED 21) ON HIS WEDDING DAY, FEBRUARY 10, 1966

FAR RIGHT, PROMO BILLBOARD ON THE ROAD TO OCHO RIOS

young Cedella Malcolm, Captain (as she called him) cut a fine figure as he rode his horse around the area.

Captain Marley was well-liked by the villagers of Nine Miles, and was a long-time friend of Cedella's father, Omeriah Malcolm. By Miss Marley's account, the short, slim, white soldier had had his eye on her for some time before seducing her when she was only 16 years old, in the small house that the Captain—who Cedella remembers as "very handsome, very loving, very sweet"—rented from her grandmother, YaYa.

Robert Nesta Marley was conceived one seemingly ordinary night in early May. "He told me he loved me

A t first glance, Nine Miles, in St Ann, Jamaica, the birthplace of Bob Marley, is nothing out of the ordinary. But then look again, and listen closely for the "natural mystic" that really does run through the air, and this typical Jamaican village of brightly-painted, one-room board houses, perched on a hillside nine miles from nowhere, starts to feel different.

In 1944, Jamaica was still a colony, and Captain Norval Marley, a middle-aged white Jamaican of the British West India Regiment, was stationed in the parish of St Ann. Then, as now, a white man in rural Jamaica was a rarity and to

"When the root is strong, the fruit is sweet"

– Bob Marley

and I believed he did," says Cedella of the Captain, who wed her in a short service held on her grandmother's veranda eight months before her baby's expected birth.

The day after the wedding, the Captain departed for Kingston, coming back to Nine Miles only a couple of times to see the "straight-nosed" mulatto baby boy who had been born on February 6, 1945, in the little house up on the hill that he had purchased for his young bride.

After a rather idyllic first few years in the never-ending children's playing-field that is rural Jamaica, Marley's father came back into his life to take him, as is the norm for many Jamaicans, to boarding school in Kingston. A photograph taken just after he left home, shows the young, brown Marley boy with his hair in a very British side-parting, a visual reminder of the two quite different cultures he had been created from.

For several months after Nesta had left home, Cedella didn't hear a thing from either husband or son. Then, she recounts, an acquaintance saw the six-year-old playing on a Kingston street. Mrs Marley's trip to town to find Nesta resulted in her taking him back to the country, discovering him as she did, not at boarding school, but on the streets of downtown Kingston where he had been living with an old lady named Miss Grey. A year or so later, Marley would move back to town with his mother, a move very difficult for him at the time, but one which would prove critical to his destiny.

As the johncrows fly, Nine Miles and Trench Town are a mere 80 miles apart, but worlds apart in culture and living conditions. Nesta had a hard time fitting in – "country come a town" say Jamaicans to sum up the shock. But, as childhood gave way to adolescence, Nesta grew comfortable with the ghetto ("too comfortable," his mother would later lament), where his friendship with two other country "bwoys" was about to give him one hell of a future.

KINGSTON 13

Judge Not   **Simmer Down**   **Ben' Down Low**

I'm Still Waiting   **Put It On**

EARLY SINGLES

1967

Around the time of the late Fifties and early Sixties, Jamaican music was just beginning to bubble. Opportunities to cut a tune for the ruling producers of the day abounded. Nesta Marley, and his longtime friend Neville Livingston (who later would become "Bunny Wailer"), along with other budding talents of the area like Desmond Dekker, teamed up together (while Marley's mother, Cedella, teamed up with "Taddy", Livingston's father) and started to get gigs in local bars with the intention of getting tight enough for the recording studio. But as Marley's dreams of a future in music grew stronger daily, his mother, in the way of many of her generation, was steering him towards a "real" job—welding.

Mrs Booker's version of this short-lived apprenticeship has it ending with Bob's eye injury on the job. Marley's own version has the eye injury happening to Desmond Dekker (who'd followed him to the welding yard). Either way, it was a fortuitous injury for both of them. As Marley told it, "The days him (Dekker) have off him check out Beverley's (production company) and him do 'Honour Thy Father And Mother'… a big hit in Jamaica. After that him say, 'come man'."

From the beginning, Chinese Jamaicans have had a strong hand in the island's pop music industry, and restauranteur, Leslie Kong, was one of the first "Chineys" to set up shop—naming his label "Beverley's" after the restaurant he operated, with his brother, in downtown Kingston (and which also served as a legal front for a Chinese numbers game). Kong was enticed into music production by a young and eager James Chambers (soon rechristened by Kong as Jimmy Cliff). Cliff, in turn, told his friends, including Desmond Dekker, about Kong. Marley, encouraged by Dekker, soon also found his way to Federal Records (Kong's production base) which was a mere couple of miles from Trench Town, and which Rita Marley would buy in 1985 and turn into Tuff Gong.

Neither Marley nor Kong ever saw their relationship as anything but business. In fact, when Kong died at 38, it was widely believed that his death was due not to a heart attack as officially reported, but to an obeah (voodoo) curse put on him by Bob for releasing an album—The Best Of The Wailers—without permission. As intriguing as this obeah story is, Bunny Wailer dismisses it angrily, as he dismisses other obeah rumours, as "an outright lie". What remains unchallenged, however, is the fact that Bob Marley didn't like Leslie Kong.

Unlike later producers of Marley's work like Coxsone Dodd and Lee "Scratch" Perry, Leslie Kong is not known for having a serious ear for music, nor did he have any technical capability in the studio. But even when relegated to the role of financial backer, Leslie Kong certainly had a feel for which artists to back. And Randall Grass, founder of Shanachie Records has written of Kong's "ear for quality", noting that, contrary to popular opinion, he did have a signature sound.

Allowing that Kong lacked "Perry's depth" and "Dodd's innovation", Grass credits Kong—who would one day oversee the Paul Simon Mother And Child Reunion sessions at Dynamic Studios— with "stripping the music down to gimmick-free formulaic essentials". And no one can deny Kong's instinct for business. He was the first investor in Chris Blackwell's Island Records, a risky but ultimately very profitable decision that he unfortunately never lived to enjoy.

'Judge Not', and the other song that was recorded at that first session, 'Do You Still Love Me?', were released both in Jamaica and Europe (the latter release, significantly by Chris Blackwell whose fate would be so intertwined with Marley's) under the artist name, "Bob Morely" (the way many Jamaicans pronounce "Marley"). Kong also tried to get Marley to change his name to "Bobby Martell" (à la Bobby Rydell), but although at least one record would go out under that pseudonym, fortunately the idea didn't stick.

Kong would produce five other tracks with Marley as a solo singer before Bob became a part of The Wailers, and temporarily parted company with his original producer—reportedly for non-payment of recording fees owing to him for two tunes.

About the same time that Marley's mother gave up the constant battle for survival on Kingston's cold and calculating streets and began planning a move to the United States, Bob Marley and Bunny Wailer linked up

> "Me grew up in the country, in the woods —to the city, ya know. A place named St Ann. They call it the garden parish. An' me grow in Kingston an' live in Trench Town from 1958 to 1961"
> – Bob Marley

NATTY THREADS,
BUNNY, BOB AND
PETER IN THE SLICK
SUITS BOUGHT FOR THEM
BY COXSONE DODD

with fellow Trench Town teen, Peter McIntosh. Tosh (his abbreviation) was, like the other two, a country boy. Born in the small fishing village of Belmont, Westmoreland, close to Negril, he moved to West Street in Trench Town from another Kingston address, when the aunt who had been his surrogate mother (his real mother having given him up shortly after birth) died. Marley, Wailer and Tosh had known each other, and had been jamming together for a while— "we used to sit in the back of Trench Town and sing"—but only became a formal group (with

Junior Braithwaite and two back-up singers) when singer Joe Higgs, later hailed as the "Godfather of Reggae", started to take an interest in them.

"Higgs," said Marley, "taught me many things," and the reggae star's mentor doesn't mind being remembered most for being Bob Marley's teacher, as long as his own contribution to reggae is acknowledged. As he says, when the Fifties ended and the Sixties (a creative decade for music worldwide) began, Kingston's burgeoning population of musicians was sensing the birth of something that was, in Higgs' words, "a new era… where the music wouldn't be 'do-overs' (covers), but songs that we wrote ourselves". To assist in this development, Higgs, though he never intended to be a teacher, set up teaching shop in his Trench Town yard. His students included The Wailers. Higgs taught all three the "rudiments of music… pitch and harmony structure… I helped them with everything. It was difficult to get the group to be precise in their sound… it took a couple of years to get it perfect."

It was also Higgs who, along with percussionist Alvin "Seeco" Patterson, set The Wailers up with Clement "Coxsone" Dodd, who, 40 years later, is still in the music business in Brooklyn, NY.

Dodd's role in the formative years of the island's music was major. Reviled by many, because of his lingering reputation for ripping off a number of great, yet naive artists in the days when doing a tune for a "'ducer" for a few pounds was seen as fair exchange, Dodd, through his fabled Studio One, is also revered as the man most instrumental in turning the strong but scattered energy of Kingston's young music scene into a full-fledged, unstoppable force.

Dodd began producing after several years of owning "sets"— the traveling, open-air discos that have always played a critical role in the island's entertainment options, as well as being a prime vehicle for the exposure of new recording artists. These sets, or sound systems, travel, with huge, 50,000-watt banks of speakers, not only to city venues but also from town to town to give rural residents a trendy and cheap night out (admission runs from JA$50.00 to $100.00, roughly US$1.50 to $2.50). Dodd, while not the first to operate a system, is generally credited with fathering the modern form of this uniquely Jamaican phenomenon by creating the "selector", the man (there are still no women) who not only spins the records but who also "toasts" (raps) in between and over the rhythms. The best of these selectors have become dancehall stars in their own right. "I came up with the idea, with my DJ, that we should rap with the people," says Dodd. It was an idea that stuck.

From his involvement with the sound systems, Dodd notes that when rock'n'roll took over from R&B as the First World's cool music of choice, Jamaicans (who have never taken to rock) were ready for a new music form of their own. Astute entrepreneur that he was, Dodd seized the opportunity to move into recording with artists like Ken Boothe, Alton Ellis, Toots And The Maytals, Burning Spear, The Soulettes (Rita Marley's group), and Marcia Griffiths (later one-third of the I'Threes, Marley's backing vocalists). In the process, he became one of the most influential, and certainly the most prolific, of Jamaican producers.

But Bob Marley, as Dodd saw it, was more than just another artist on the Studio One roster. "Bob was with me for about five years. He lived at the back of the studio (in a small room that Bob strongly believed to be haunted) and I sort of adopted him because his mother wasn't here." Dodd also admits to being the first to separate Bob from The Wailers (a significant switch which Chris Blackwell would later be blamed for), because he sensed that he "was the one". But the fact that along the way some titles were released as "Peter Tosh and The Wailers", suggests that it was more often just a case of who was on lead vocals.

In The Wailers' first Studio One incarnation, the group included Junior Braithwaite, and Beverley Kelso and Cherry Smith, the two back-ups. But this sextet was quickly pared down to what Bunny Wailer calls the "no baggage Wailers".

Jamaica in the early Sixties was in transition from colony to free state and when the power shift came in 1962, it was marked on August 5 by a euphoric, midnight ceremony attended by HRH Princess Margaret—who would return to Jamaica in 1997, as a guest of Chris Blackwell, staying at the now Blackwell-owned Ian Fleming estate, GoldenEye—her then husband, the Earl of Snowden, and Lyndon Baines Johnson, vice president (to President John F Kennedy) of the United States. Independence brought with it a vitality that invigorated, albeit temporarily) all aspects of Jamaican life. Music especially benefited from this new free spirit, and it is no coincidence that the beginning of the nation's musical identity commenced with its severing of colonial ties.

Clement Coxsone Dodd, after signing The Wailers to a tight five-year production/management deal, scored a hit with their third Studio One recording, 'Simmer Down', a rollicking, ska survival anthem that featured a backing band made up of some of Jamaica's best musicians, including the internationally renowned trombonist, the late Don Drummond.

In the wake of this hit, Dodd began to groom his group in earnest, outfitting them in the slim-fitting mohair and lamé suits so favored by US R&B groups of the Fifties, and putting them on a £3 a week salary.

As the owner of several sound systems, Dodd was in the enviable position of having instant access to the public ear.

> ## "The only truth is Rastafari"
> — Bob Marley

Jamaican radio was, and remains, resistant to anything new or different, and without these outdoor sessions, much of this daring and disturbing (to uptowners) music emerging from the ghetto would never have been exposed. Dodd also—and in this he was way ahead of his time—used his sets to popularize his acts, sending them around the country to perform with his Downbeat set.

For the young Wailers, 1964 was a big year. In February, 'Simmer Down' hit Number One, and the group was consistently in the charts for the rest of the year. Many of these first Wailers recordings have stood the test of considerable time, remarkable in light of the fact that when Dodd first opened Studio One (after first experimenting in production at Ken Khouri's Federal Records Studio), he only had a one-track tape machine bought from Federal when Khouri upgraded to a two-track. Dodd later purchased the two-track when Federal

KINGSTON, JAMAICA,
THE INDEPENDENCE
CELEBRATIONS MARKED
THE END OF 300 YEARS
OF BRITISH RULE

invested in an eight-track. And, like the output of most of his peers, Dodd's productions were almost all "one-take"—or, "run tune and done".

As Jamaican music took on a form of its own, so did its religion. Rastafarianism, which first emerged in the early Thirties, suddenly began to spread rapidly and became the religion of choice for the disenfranchised and forgotten people of the shanty towns which were, in the first flush of the island's independence, more than ready for a new Messiah, especially a black one.

The Rasta movement, with its worship of Emperor Haile Selassie I of Ethiopia based much of its philosophy on the back-to-Africa teachings of black orator and entrepreneur Marcus Mosiah Garvey (he formed the ill-fated Black Star Line, the name obviously a take-off on Cunard's mammoth White Star Line), who, like Marley, came from the parish of St Ann. However, it was not until Rasta and reggae music—which took over from ska and rocksteady —merged that the religion became such a powerful and influential phenomenon.

"The only truth is Rastafari," said Marley, who would also describe his faith as "not a culture", but a "reality".

The reality of Rastafari was first shown to Marley while he was with Dodd. Many of Coxsone's musicians were already sprouting locks and sporting the red, green and gold African identity of the Rastaman. Peter Tosh and

Bunny Wailer were similarly intrigued. Rastafari appealed most to the rebels in society, those who questioned the socio-political system. Besides, the teachings of Rasta couldn't be properly ingested without generous helpings of herb (all the better to meditate), a perk that gave Jah Rastafari a serious edge over the traditional church.

As it turned out, Rasta wouldn't just appeal to the blacks of the Diaspora for whom its message was originally intended, but also to the vast population of white "hippies" (or those of kindred mind) left over from the Sixties.

The anti-system stance of Rastafari, coupled with its emphasis on natural living, and a world future of peace, love and unity was attractive enough, but add to that a little intoxicating sensimillia and a "killer riddim" and who could resist?

Having locksed and "trimmed" twice (at his mother's request) before making a final commitment to Rastafari when he came back to Jamaica from the US, Marley had mulled over his conversion for a long time in light of the "outlaw" status conferred on followers of the faith by the conservative majority of Jamaicans. But, once he had fully accepted Jah as "earth's rightful ruler", he quickly became the movement's most visible and powerful exponent (a role for which no successor has ever been found).

Sorry that he had been off the island during the April 1966 visit of Haile Selassie, a visit treasured by the Rastafarian community (despite the Emperor's vehement denials of divinity, and his brief panic attack, which sent him scurrying back inside the plane when he first saw the vast sea of welcoming dreadlocks), he began a significant association with Rasta elder Mortimer Planner shortly after his return from America in October. Planner would continue as Marley's spiritual adviser and friend for many years.

Bob's spiritual beliefs became more entrenched, and his focus changed from love songs to message music, producers like Dodd, Kong and, later, American Danny Sims, shied away from recording the songs with serious lyrics. Sims especially wanted to keep Marley playing as much R&B mainstream as possible to penetrate the US market.

Danny Sims had met The Wailers in 1967, when he and singer Johnny Nash came to Kingston to record a new Nash album. The decision to produce in Jamaica had been made primarily to cut costs—Jamaican studio rates then being far cheaper than those of comparable international rooms—but Sims soon realized that the island was a place for good songs. He was especially impressed by Marley's writing and commissioned him to write songs for Nash (two of which, 'Stir It Up' and 'Guava Jelly' would become US pop hits. He also signed the three Wailers to a production and publishing deal (with JAD Records and Cayman Publishing), putting them all on a modest living allowance of $100 a week each.

The Wailers recorded almost 90 songs for Sims and it was these songs that would form the basis of the 1999 release, *The Complete Bob Marley 1967 to 1972*. Heralded by the international press as equal to "stumbling on Picasso's complete Cubist works", in Jamaica, the collection was accorded customary, and slightly cynical, nonchalence.

Sims has also been accused of releasing demo tracks never intended for public hearing. When *Chances Are* was released by Sims in 1982, Blackwell was dismayed and accused the major label that released it of cynical exploitation. The same reception was given to JAD's next release, *Bob Marley*.

The practise of releasing albums made up of various singles that The Wailers' first producers had recorded began early. Leslie Kong released *The Best Of The Wailers* (Beverley's), as did Dodd in two volumes (Studio One and Buddha), prompting a furious Marley to complain that "the best" hadn't happened yet.

Both of these albums were then re-released under different titles, a devious practise that hasn't gone away.

Dodd also put out *The Wailing Wailers* (Studio One), *Marley, Tosh And Livingston* (Studio One), *The Birth Of A Legend* (Calla and CBS), *Early Music—Bob Marley And The Wailers* featuring *Peter Tosh* (CBS), and *Bob Marley And The Wailers with Peter Tosh* (Hallmark).

Danny Sims entered the picture later but caught up quickly, releasing *Soul Rebel* (New Cross) before *Chances Are* (Cotillion).

> "To this day, the only legal way out of the ghetto for many of its yout' is through 'the music'"
> **– Bob Marley**

RASTAMEN RULE ETERNAL—A SIGN OF THE SEVENTIES

JUDGE NOT

A uditioning this song *a cappella* for Kong, the teen-aged Nesta Marley, while not earning the producer's praise, did impress enough for him to "get through"—Jamaican parlance for getting what you want: in this case, Bob Marley's first outing on wax. The year was 1961.

'Judge Not', a ska single released on Kong's Beverley's label didn't make much of a dent anywhere, and would have vanished without regret had its singer not had a destiny unimaginable at the time.

"It nevah really do nuttin', but it a good song still," said Marley about his freshman recording effort after he became a star. Others weren't as complimentary, citing the song's distinctive penny whistle as irritating.

Leslie Kong, whose biggest hit as producer was Desmond Dekker's Seventies' smash, 'The Israelites' (which Jews the world over interpreted as being about them, when in fact it was an early call to the black Diaspora), recorded his artists at Federal Studio owned by Syrian, Ken Khouri, on Marcus Garvey Drive. Khouri, another Jamaican music pioneer was the first to offer (in 1954) recording and pressing at one location—a couple of decades later, Tuff Gong, Marley's own facility, would occupy premises and offer similar services after the complex was bought by his widow to house the manufacturing and distribution facilities formerly based on Hope Road.

The relationship between producer and artist was tenuous from the outset. As Bob told it: "I meet Leslie Kong at Federal… and that man rude. Tell me sing my song straight out standing outside… him tek me inna room, past Chinaman, and this guy (Ken Khouri) who tek the money… so I sang (and) say to him, 'what if it a hit?'… then man a name a Dowling mek me sign the release form dem, den push me outta studio."

There are conflicting reports of what Marley got paid for his first session. His mother remembers it as £5 out of which she got £2 ("he always made sure his Mama got her cut"), her sister, Enid, ten shillings, and a friend, five, leaving her son with £2.10 (the same amount as her weekly housekeeping wage). Don Taylor, who later managed Marley, recounts it as £20, a figure that Bob himself confirmed by saying he got two £10 notes. Whatever the exact amount (and the math doesn't seem to add up entirely), Kong got a bargain.

'Judge Not'/'Do You Still Love Me?' was released internationally in 1963 in London by a young British-born white Jamaican, Christopher Blackwell, who, a decade later, released *Catch A Fire*, The Wailers first album on his own Island Records label, and who would be the man commonly credited with giving Bob Marley to the world.

I'M STILL WAITING

F rom a lyrical perspective, 'I'm Still Waiting' is not one of Bob Marley's best, but this song is significant in that it was recorded at the first Studio One session, along with 'It Hurts To Be Alone' (written and sung by Junior Braithwaite). The song is also significant for its beautiful, haunting vocal (once you get past the kitsch opening bars). Owing much to the harmony arrangements of popular R&B groups of the day, the production is original enough to hold the ear,

> "Jamaicans go slow, everything is soon come, but if there's one thing they rush about it's making a recordin'… them guys killer of reggae music"
>
> **– Bob Marley**

and the emotion of the singer captures the listener over and over again. Some have speculated that the slight lag between singer and musicians was intentional, but with Coxsone's studio being a one-track facility, that would have been impossible. The more prosaic technical explanation, according to engineer Barry O'Hare, without knowing whose track was being analysed, is that the singer was behind the rhythm.

'I'm Still Waiting' was one of a string of hits that the group had in 1966, for which they each reportedly got only £60, angering Marley to the point where, before thinking better of it, he considered taking up a gun and "going down there to blast away. These (producers) put out 200 songs a year with 60 different labels and 900 different singers… Jamaicans go slow, everything is 'soon come', but if there's one thing Jamaicans rush about it's making a recordin'… them guys killer of reggae music." The sad thing about Marley's astute observations—made about 20 years ago—is that nothing, really, has changed.

SIMMER DOWN

The deceptively simple lyrics of 'Simmer Down', The Wailers' first Jamaican hit, are as relevant to the fires of discontent that burn in downtown Kingston today as they were when Bob Marley wrote the lyrics in the Sixties. "The battle (would) get hotter," he predicted—and it has.

Recorded for Coxsone Dodd, 'Simmer Down' spoke to the endemic social unrest of urban Jamaica as no other song before it. Many of the musicians on this Studio One session are now dead, and Dodd's Brentford Road studio, long out of vogue, was recently dismantled and the equipment advertised for sale. Guitarist and arranger of the song, Ernie Ranglin, now in his sixties, speaks bitterly of the experience. "I don't remember anything about those times," he says. "I wanted to forget everything that happened… people made their money off it… let them remember." Dodd's session musicians were paid a paltry £2 a tune, so perhaps Ranglin's regrets, in the light of the millions made from the song, aren't surprising.

'Simmer Down', first aired only hours after it was recorded on Dodd's sound system, was released on the Coxsone label just before Christmas in 1963, and was a bona fide Jamaican hit by February of the following year (even if, as myth has it, The Wailers had to personally go to the radio stations and threaten the DJs with death if they didn't play it—a more direct and less expensive method to ensure airplay than the present-day "payola".

The first live rendition of the track, and supposedly the group's first public performance, was given at a talent show at the Majestic Theatre. The Wailers won over the traditionally tough Jamaican audience with what was described by singer Alton Ellis as this "different kind of music", but didn't win the contest—provoking what was later reported as an all-out brawl between Marley and the night's victors, the long-forgotten Uniques.

But the hit had its critics. As Bunny Wailer, downplaying the song's significance points out, the melody wasn't original and the track didn't earn The Wailers the respect of their peers. "It was a nursery rhyme song, something that people heard every day, a nursery rhyme that is sung in schoolyards, in back yards, but that was the record that hit. So… people didn't rate the record. They said to us you didn't do any record, don't take that for nuttin', you're lucky. You better make sure and record one we want to hear, some serious lyrics."

Nursery rhyme or not, 'Simmer Down' got The Wailers noticed. It also got them a regular recording gig with Dodd, who as well as advancing money for slick stage clothes, put the trio on a weekly wage of £3 each (recoupable of course). For the first time, The Wailers were living—if modestly—off their musical works.

RITA MARLEY WITH THE MARLEY KIDS.

PUT IT ON

This Coxsone Dodd-produced ska record was played repeatedly at Bob and Rita's, humble— yet by the bride's account very happy—home wedding on February 10, 1966. On February 11 (like his father before him who had left Marley's mother the day after their wedding), Marley left Rita for Delaware. The grainy black-and-white photo taken that day shows a young, happy and very ordinary couple, blissfully unaware that they were about to embark on a very extraordinary life.

The former Rita Anderson had met Bob in the lanes that led from Trench Town to Studio One on Brentford Road. The Wailers had to pass close to Rita's house (where she lived with her Aunt Viola) to get to the studio, and the nursing student-cum-singer (she had dreams, too), had wangled a meeting, getting to know the trio better when her vocal group, The Soulettes, made their way to Studio One. Although Rita, who was already the mother of one-year-old Sharon, had first gravitated towards Peter Tosh, she then switched focus

BEN' DOWN LOW

'Ben' Down Low' was a Number One in Jamaica, but they were "pressin' it, sellin' it… a black market type a business", said Marley of the song that reaped them no royalties and precipitated The Wailers' split with Dodd and Studio One. 'Ben' Down Low' was the first song produced after Marley's return to JA following one of his two brief working stints in middle America. "Me come back a Jamaica an' do 'Ben' Down Low', which was a hit an' dem rob we out of it again. We come back with 'Nice Time', but man is all robbery… rob you down to nuttin'."

A perfect dance tune, 'Ben' Down Low' is a descriptive phrase for all Jamaican styles of dance from African-inspired folk to today's raunchy dancehall, but never was it used more effectively than in this catchy ska tune, which will still get any Jamaican over 40 on the dance-floor in seconds.

> "Me come back a Jamaica an' do 'Ben' Down Low', which was a hit an' dem rob we out of it again. We come back with 'Nice Time', but man is all robbery... rob you down to nuttin'"
>
> **– Bob Marley**

to Bob (stirring, some say, the first jealousy between the two men). 'Put It On' was recorded during the couple's first months together, and thus was a fitting theme song to celebrate their marriage.

Bob's mother, in her book, *Bob Marley*, doesn't paint as sweet a picture of Bob's marriage which, she says, her son denied, putting the whole event down to the conjuring of a "Madda" (obeah woman) who kissed his hand, "and the next thing he knew he was married to Rita". Others, like Don Taylor, add to the speculation by reporting that Rita's Aunt Viola (who Bob was said to fear), was an obeah woman.

BOB, PETER AND BUNNY

THE INFAMOUS LEE 'SCRATCH' PERRY DEFINED THE WAILERS' SOUND IN THE STUDIO

1971

The next producer to enter the picture was Lee "Scratch" Perry. It was Perry who defined The Wailers' reggae sound, bringing out the bass as a lead instrument and pulling from Bob and the other Wailers, lead vocals that have an ethereal quality that could penetrate the hardest heart.

Everybody in Jamaican music has a Lee "Scratch" Perry tale to tell. There was the time he covered his Black Ark Studio (both inside and out) with tiny "X's" (it took several weeks); the time he appeared at a memorial concert for seminal reggae producer Jack Ruby, dressed in a red and white satin suit and hat, as *Alice In Wonderland*'s Mad Hatter, with a very tall, buxom blonde on his arm; the time he was spotted outside Nassau's Compass Point Studio tuning the grey, static screen of a broken television "to outer space"; and the time he crushed a red brick to mud in his Bahamas bathroom and left it for a very unhappy maid to clean up. Debate about the authenticity of his madness continues and it's said that he once feigned madness to thwart gunmen who were after him, and then the hoax stuck. But, fact or fiction, no other individual, has added as many colourful stories to Kingston's musical lore as Perry.

Apart from being gossipworthy, Perry is very good at what he does. Chris Blackwell is one of a number of people who give Perry the credit for producing The Wailers' best material. This even though it was the music Blackwell had a hand in that broke the band internationally. "Lee Perry had an incredible feel," Blackwell says. "A kind of magic… Perry was one of the master music people I believe."

Perry began his production career with Coxsone Dodd as the Downbeat Sound System's rankin' selector. He then moved into engineering and production at Studio One, starting his own production company when he tired of toiling long hours for Coxsone's alleged low pay. The Wailers was one of the first acts he produced and Perry, unlike Kong and Dodd, remained friends with Marley, despite some serious spats.

The Wailers stopped working with Dodd shortly after 'Bus' Dem Shut' was released. "The man rob we," said Bob, a common refrain of artists of that time who sold their art for small sums simply to survive. But, as Chris Blackwell points out, it was their choice. "The way it was done then is that everyone wanted a flat fee (regretting it when they found out that there was

money to be made on the back end). There was no real industry… and when there is no royalty system in place, it always makes sense to sell something outright." He goes on to note that the producers were "not really taking advantage of the artists, it was the only logical way of dealing with it".

What Blackwell denounces is the practice by some Jamaican producers of not compensating these artists properly when old tracks got new life and royalties were reaped on the rebounds. During another interview Blackwell says that because royalties were not being paid to The Wailers on any of their early material, he had suggested to them that they re-cut many of the songs recorded for those first producers and re-claim the publishing and other rights that had been taken away from them.

Royalty issues aside, however, The Wailers worked well with Scratch Perry (and dealt well with idiosyncrasies like Perry's preference for recording in "mono" because he believed in the "unity of one" and that stereo had a split personality).

On songs like 'Duppy Conqueror', 'Soul Almighty', 'Try Me', 'Cornerstone', 'Kaya' and 'Small Axe', Perry not only pared away the excess from The Wailers' sound, he also created a tension and mood in the group's music that Marley carried forward into his later work.

Perry's production of The Wailers coincided with the birth of reggae—what Bob Marley called "earth feelin' music". The short era of rock-steady, which ruled after ska, was already giving way to the hypnotic "riddim" that would take Jamaican music to every place on the planet—the music's addictive power and worldwide appeal due in part to the music of Robert Nesta Marley, but also a reflection of the high level of creative energy that was surging out of Kingston during those early times. Sly Dunbar describes this period as "wicked—there was live music everywhere and the studios were full all the time".

Mr Perry not only gave The Wailers a more distinct

> "We were so much in love with the music and with what we were doing that money could not come between us and that music"
>
> **– Bunny Wailer**

sound, he also gave them—albeit unwittingly—the musicians who would become first a part of the original Wailers, and then a couple of years down the road Marley's backing band. Drum and bass brothers, Carlton (Carly) and Aston (Family Man) Barrett, who were the rhythm section of Perry's house band, The Upsetters, would, along with Bob on rhythm guitar, Peter on keys and lead guitar, and Bunny on percussion, become the new Wailers band in good time for the first Island album, *Catch A Fire*.

Marley never saw himself as much of a musician, but said that when session players, tired of being ripped off by producers, protested by not being available for sessions, The Wailers had no choice but to "start playin' ourselves". Bassist, Family Man Barrett, who met Bob at The Wailers' second retail record shop on Orange Street, "where he used to sit outside and reason, sometimes for the whole day", taught Marley most of what he

knew about guitar. "He used to say that he could have been a better guitar player, but 'Family Man won't teach me any more chords'."

To call the mid- to late-Sixties the golden age of Jamaican music is an understatement. On every street corner sat a songwriter. And at every studio gate stood a long line of hopefuls, each with a surefire hit song for any producer who would bite. If the singer impressed the producer enough to get called into the studio, the routine was simple and swift. "We would line up and sing a tune a cappella," says Junior Tucker, who began singing professionally at the age of five, "so that the keyboard player could get the chords." Then the bass player would find a line, and the drummer catch a groove and the rhythm track was laid. The vocalist had a maximum of two takes to lay down a decent vocal. "Every man haffi come sharp," is how Tucker puts it, noting that

PRODUCER JOE GIBBS' RECORD SHOP ON NEW KINGSTON.

for those who couldn't make it, there was always a "ring-master" like Robbie Shakespeare ready to show them to the door. "Robbie would lick their back with his bass if they didn't move out fast enough," Tucker laughs, describing these sessions as "a makeshift little factory". As he tells it, "half of the equipment didn't work, and at Channel One there was even a hole in the wall, but they'd just plug up the hole or push in a bit of paper to hold a loose plug, and go again."

Somehow out of this chaos came perfection. And the musicians knew it. It was the reason Bob Marley would later "allow the madness at 56 Hope Road" say several of those who were part of it, and the reason people like Sly and Robbie continue to record at sessions jampacked with people "hanging in" or "passing through". Says Sly: "It's the vibes."

"Harry J's studio was known for the vibes," says Cat Coore, lead guitar player for the band, Third World, who were recording at Harry J's at the same time as The Wailers. "It wasn't the best in terms of equipment," says Coore. "It had its little quirks, but Harry J is a good man

and everyone liked recording there."

The Wailers had moved to Harry Johnson's Roosevelt Avenue studio (which also offered pressing and distribution) as they got better at their craft, feeling —despite a lot of disagreement from various producers and other musicians who remained loyal to the earlier studios—that they were getting a better sound there than what they could get at any of the earlier, downtown rooms (though Dynamics continued to be the studio of choice for many and The Wailers would also use it intermittently).

Unlike those first studios, Harry J's was uptown, just a short drive away from the town's two main hotels, the Jamaica Pegasus, and the then Kingston Sheraton (which until 1984 was the only place in Jamaica with an escalator). "When Harry J's opened for us ghetto people," says Tucker, "it was a revelation. It was Jamaica's first well-run studio. It had a receptionist, and most important," he says, remembering it differently to Coore, "everything worked." Harry J's was also the first studio which had been set up more for recording albums than singles.

Harry J's clients were more likely to block book time, than to come for a little three-hour session.

As for Harry J himself, who has always felt that his contribution to Jamaica's music and to the production of The Wailers has never been fully recognized, he was a man who had enough vision to realise that reggae could reach the rest of the world and to produce music that although considered "soft" at the time by the hardcore set, continued, like The Wailers' music, to bridge the gap between local reggae and international pop. 'Bed's Too Big' by Sheila Hylton is a good example of his work—and one which was mocked by Jamaican purists incensed that a Jamaican producer had done a cover of a "white reggae" tune, until the song was a big hit in England that is. The consensus now is that Harry J was a remarkable producer with a good sense of sound whose role in the development of Jamaican music and the success of The Wailers was, as Harry J has always claimed, vastly underrated.

Marley's studio habits were formed very early on. A stickler for punctuality—"He was always the first one on the tour bus," says Chris Blackwell—and military-like precision, he was a man on a God-given mission who had no time to waste, especially studio time that he was paying for. His music, and his message, were his life, and taken more seriously than anything else, including his women.

> **"... there was live music everywhere and the studios were full all the time"**
>
> **– Sly Dunbar**

But Bunny, Peter and Bob were still very much a trio at this point in The Wailers' career. And Bunny and Peter shared Marley's commitment to solid production.

Bunny Wailer sums up that magical time: "We were so much in love with the music and with what we were doing that money could not come between us and that music.

"Money couldn't get near. That's why these guys were always creaming and ripping us off, because The Wailers weren't worried about money. We were trying to build our artistry so that when we heard what we'd done we'd be satisfied." But, says Bunny, The Wailers didn't stay satisfied for long. "The Wailers' design was always to improve… every member of The Wailers was like that. You could hear it in the work."

In 1966, The Wailers established Wail N Soul M. In 1969, Tuff Gong Export was taken as a trade name to distinguish the records that were being sent abroad. In 1970, they opened a Tuff Gong shop on Orange Street, which then moved to 127 King Street and, in 1973, the name was formalised via incorporation, first as Tough Gang Records, and then changed a month later to Tuff Gong Records Limited. Each of The Wailers received 1,331 shares. Tuff Gong—a symbol of what once was—would continue to be The Wailers' label for some time after the musical alliance broke up, but then fell dormant until it was reactivated in 1983 by Bunny Wailer. He ran a full-page ad in Jamaica's *Daily Gleaner* in 1996, denouncing the fact that Chris Blackwell had quietly attempted to appropriate the name in 1990 (and apparently succeeded).

BUS' DEM SHUT (PYAKA)

Produced by The Wailers at Dynamics in 1966, and released on their Wail N Soul M label as The Wailing Wailers, the short-lived variant on their original name, this recording pretty well sums up what they were beginning to feel from certain quarters of society. A "pyaka" is an envious person and "to cut down pyakaism" is a plea to let go of the envy and work together, a plea still being aired daily in this land where covetousness is said to be the national malaise. Jealousy is prevalent everywhere, but in Jamaica it is especially vicious. Were it not for this dark side to the national psyche, it is strongly believed that many of Jamaica's ills would be resolved.

"Jamaica is a place," said Bob, "where you really build up competition in your mind. People here feel they must fight against me and I must fight against you… Jealousy. Suspicion. Anger. Poverty. Competition. We should just get together and create music."

SCREWFACE

Bob Marley was known, like his father, to be a serious "screwface" (someone with an angry or mean expression), and had a nasty temper which exploded whenever anyone (especially one of his women) tested his patience. Intimates knew when to steer clear of him and not test The Skipper. But the screwface the song speaks of is not Bob—it's the screwface in society who is always there, waiting, watching and knowing who to frighten and Marley telling "Jah Jah children" to fear no foe—as long as their faith remains rooted in Jah they will be protected.

Another self-produced single (at Harry J's and Randy's), this was recorded in 1971, during the Lee Perry and JAD days.

ONE CUP OF COFFEE

Native Jamaicans—who grow some of the world's best—don't drink coffee (although the mention of it in early folk songs suggests that at one time they did drink the beverage, but in breakfast bowls rather than cups). The British, who were still in Jamaica when the song was written didn't drink it either. And, unlike today when other cultures of the world are finally penetrating this insular island via cable television, in the Sixties Jamaican culture would never have stretched to incorporate a concept like "one cup of coffee and then I'll go". The idea for the lyric most likely came from one of the foreign films that were shown at the open-air movie theatres dotted around the island, which served as a popular entertainment centre and meeting place for the island's teenagers until the mid-Eighties (Kingstonians didn't have to sit in the open air—they had the grand, and enclosed Carib

Theatre, where live music alternated with films, and groups like The Wailers had frequent gigs). Even the song's reference to bringing the money to his woman "like the lawyer said he should do", sounds very Hollywood-inspired, given the total lack of legally enforced child support in the country at that time.

Leslie Kong put this single out on his Beverley's label under the bland stage name, "Bobby Martell", the producer saying at the time that "Nesta Marley" wasn't marketable. Although the first recording of 'One Cup Of Coffee' was a straight-ahead ska version, later covers of the song have shown its versatility and staying power. Son Damian (by Cindy Breakespeare), Bob Marley's youngest child, who is now a DJ named Junior Gong, showed, in the "do over" of this track he did for his debut album, that it can even keep up with the dancehall/hip hop Nineties.

MELLOW MOOD

It's not a widely-known fact, but The Wailers, in between laying down tracks for Kong, Dodd, JAD Records and Perry, produced many tunes themselves. Recorded at Dynamics with Clancy Eccles in 1966, and put out as the flipside of 'Ben' Down Low', 'Mellow Mood' was one of the first releases on The Wailers' newly-formed Wail N Soul M label (the logo of which featured three hands clasped together with the names "Bunnie", "Peter" and "Bob").

Wail N Soul M Records (both label and shop) was located at 18a Greenwich Park Road, where Rita had been living before she married Bob. The venture was started in 1967 with the few dollars Marley had managed to put aside from his Delaware days. Having seen how the producer/label owner (in those days it was usually the same person) controlled the profits, Marley decided early on that he must "control I destiny". That businesses need adequate financing to flourish was not something a Trench Town "rudebwoy" would realize, but the capitalist concept of maximizing profit by keeping everything under one roof was, in 1966, especially under Manley's socialist-leaning rule, well ahead of his time. Wail N Soul M went belly up pretty fast, but not before the young entrepreneurs got valuable lessons in the runnings of the music business.

'Mellow Mood' has proven to be one of the most durable of Marley's compositions, having been recorded by Judy Mowatt and many others.

JUDY MOWATT RECORDED A VERSION OF 'MELLOW MOOD'. SHE IS NO LONGER A RASTAFARIAN BUT A DEVOUT CHRISTIAN

NICE TIME

'Nice Time' is one of Jamaica's favourite "Bob tunes". Everyone knows the words to the chorus, which as well as being an expression of well-being—Marley had just come home from his winter in Wilmington—also has a more earthy interpretation.

'Nice Time' (which later became Marley's nickname for eldest daughter, Cedella), was recorded in 1967, and was one of the last Wail N Soul M releases. The making and marketing of music, The Wailers had discovered, took far more investment—of both time and money—than they had ever imagined.

Later, The Wailers recorded 'Nice Time' for Danny Sims, a duplication that became a pattern. Unlike most artists who only do one version of a song, The Wailers collectively, and Bob singularly, frequently re-recorded the same songs for different producers.

AN EARLY BOB MARLEY AND THE WAILERS, STEPPING OUT WITH MILITANT YOUT' ATTITUDE

CORNER STONE

Bob Marley had a thing about cornerstones, which are a recurring theme in his lyrics, 'Cornerstone', written in the mid-Sixties, and recorded by The Wailers for Scratch Perry, clearly shows Marley's insecurities, as well as a strong underlying belief in his own "cornerstone" value. "The stone that the builder refuse, will always be the head cornerstone," goes the song.

Rejection was always a part of Bob Marley's life, beginning with the pain he suffered by having an absentee,

and plainly uncaring, father. Later, his mother (who had always told him that "God is the father of the fatherless"), in the way of many Jamaican mothers, left him temporarily with his grandmother while she went off to find work. She also left him behind with Coxsone Dodd in Kingston when she emigrated ("migrated" as Jamaicans say) to the USA. He also feared rejection from the women he got involved with —always keeping them at a safe distance so that any rejecting that was to be done would come from him.

DUPPY CONQUEROR

A duppy is the Jamaican term for a ghost. Bob swore that there was a duppy in Coxsone's back room (where he bunked when his mother left Kingston), and wrote this song after he moved out. It also relates to the time each of The Wailers spent in jail (for specious drug and/or traffic charges), as well as the ever-present evil spirits that vie for control of this strange land, and its inhabitants, and speaks of the euphoria felt when that negative force is conquered—one of the reasons why Rastafari places an emphasis on positive thinking.

Jamaica's obeah is akin to Haiti's voodoo and Columbia's santeria, all a cross between Christianity and the ancestral beliefs of African slaves, and all used for both good and evil. It is said that all that is needed for an evil spell to have power is a person's photo, and it is not unusual in the Caribbean for perfectly rational people to sprinkle white rum in every corner of their house for protection.

Put out by Scratch Perry as 'Doppy Conqueror', in 1970, 'Duppy Conqueror' was so well-produced and performed that it still holds its own with The Wailers' Island catalogue. It was also a song that The Wailers liked playing. Seven different versions were recorded.

> "God is the father of the fatherless"

TRENCHTOWN ROCK

This was the first release on The Wailers' Tuff Gong label, which was established, on an investment of a few dollars, some three years after Wail N Soul M folded. Unlike its predecessor, Tuff Gong (one of Bob's street names) was successful from the outset. 'Trenchtown Rock' zoomed straight to the top of radio station RJR's Top 40, staying there for several weeks in the summer of 1971.

Reggae, with its potent mix of direct message and meandering melodies, gave ghetto dwellers a voice that they'd never had before. Kingston 13, which includes Trench Town, is considered the worst of addresses, and no one had ever "bigged the residents up" in song before Bob.

The subtle and socially constructive suggestion in the lyric that music can protect and empower—"You can't come

THE INTERIOR OF TUFF GONG, THE WAILERS' SHOP, SHOWCASING 'PURE BOB MARLEY MUSIC'

cold I up" (kill me)—better than the gun, because when music hits "you feel no pain", is in marked contrast to the stark negativity of 1999's "anytime mi hungry agin, dem a guh si mi nine (millimetre gun)". The latter line, taken from DJ Bounty Killa's controversial Number One song 'Anytime', sums up the downwards slide of Jamaica's music since the halcyon days of The Skipper.

HIGH TIDE OR LOW TIDE

This song was recorded in 1969. Produced by The Wailers and briefly considered for the *Catch A Fire* album, it was mixed in 1972. But 'High Tide Or Low Tide' was not released until Island Records' *Songs Of Freedom* appeared in 1992. Musically, the track misses, and is not up to the level of other Wailers work. The melody is unremarkable, the harmony is loose, and the arrangement reminiscent of second-rate R&B. It's not hard to understand why it was collectively decided to hold it back until 1992 when there was little else left that hadn't already been heard. But 'High Tide Or Low Tide' does have a memorable lyric and it could have become a beautiful song had a bit more time been spent on finding a melody that did it justice and running just one more take on the vocals.

From most reports, Bob Marley loved children and tried, despite his peripatetic lifestyle, to be a good father to all his offspring, legitimately begotten or otherwise, and to give them the protection he cites his mother as asking for in this song. Themes that allow for dual interpretation are a constant in Marley's writing and 'High Tide Or Low Tide' is a good example. The chorus is about being a good friend in both high and low seas and could apply to anyone. The verses pin it down to his being there for his children.

THE YOUNG MARLEY COUPLE WITH FAMILY. LEFT TO RIGHT, SHARON, ZIGGY, CEDELLA, AND IN CARRIAGE, STEVEN

CATCH A FIRE

Stir It Up

Slave Driver

Midnight Ravers

Concrete Jungle

Baby We've Got A Date (Rock It Baby)

No More Trouble

Kinky Reggae

Produced by: Chris Blackwell and Bob Marley

CHRIS BLACKWELL IN OCHO RIOS IN THE MID-EIGHTIES

1972

The most critical connexion in Marley's career was made in London, 1972, when The Wailers went to see Chris Blackwell, head of the independent Island Records, then one of the hottest labels in rock.

Only a barefoot island boy with good breeding—a streetwise sophisticate—could have created Island Records. Such a boy was Christopher Blackwell.

Born in London just before World War II, Blackwell was carried home to Jamaica, by boat, at the age of six months, by his Irish father, Joseph, and Jewish-Jamaican mother, Blanche. "Christopher has never forgiven me for having been born in England instead of in Jamaica," says Blanche Blackwell.

At the age of 10, like all Jamaican children of his color and class, Christopher Blackwell returned to England to attend boarding school, in his case, Harrow, which he attended for several years. A rebel and an entrepreneur even then, the 17-year-old schoolboy—after a humbling public caning—was expelled for selling liquor and cigarettes to fellow pupils.

Back in Jamaica, Chris Blackwell hung out with well-connected friends of his parents, such as Errol Flynn (who had a house in Port Antonio), and Ian Fleming (whose *GoldenEye* property in Oracabessa, Blackwell would one day buy), and got his first taste of the entertainment business as a location scout for the James Bond film, *Dr No.*

Much to his mother's distress—"I wanted Christopher to be a chartered accountant and sent him to Price Waterhouse"—Blackwell then started dabbling in music, finding a ready market in Jamaica for rare R&B 78s picked up in New York and re-sold, *sans* identifying label, for a decent profit.

Next, he went into music production for himself but finding, despite three local hits in a row, that doing business in the cut-throat Kingston market had major limitations, he decided to move back to Britain, and, instead of competing with his rivals, distribute their music overseas, which he did through a one-half interest in a company called Trojan Records.

Island Records, named from the famous Alec Waugh novel, *Island In The Sun*, was founded in 1962, the same year that the Union Jack was lowered for the last time, and the new Jamaican flag of black, green and gold (symbolizing hardship, fertility and sunshine, respectively) rose to the ecstatic cheers of a country that believed itself to be on the brink of a brilliant future. It was an exciting, if turbulent, time in the Caribbean and Blackwell fed off the raw energy that flowed from this changing order. Crossing social and color lines to understand, and absorb, the power of a music that had suddenly sprung from a people finally free from colonial restraint, Blackwell took a modest investment of £5,000 (which 30 years later would give him a $350 million return) and started his label.

His first hit, Millie Small's six million seller, 'My Boy Lollipop', came quickly, and flush with this beginner's luck, Blackwell signed a slew of British rock acts and temporarily took his attention away from the music that had got him started. Jimmy Cliff and Perry Henzell's classic film of the ghetto, *The Harder They Come*, got him back in.

For a short while, Jimmy Cliff was Island's main focus. "I was so excited about where we could go with him," says Blackwell, remembering how upset he was when he and Cliff fell out and the singer signed with EMI. But as Jimmy Cliff walked out of Island's door, Bob Marley and The Wailers walked in. "Off the street," says Blackwell.

Through his interest in Trojan Records, Blackwell had already released a few Wailers singles, including 'Simmer Down', which, at the time, he recalls, "was just another record". He even spelled Marley's name wrong. But when he met them in person he sensed that the trio had something he could work with, noting that Bob bore a striking character resemblance to Rhygin', the real-life gangster that Jimmy Cliff's role in the Henzell film was based on. "He was a combination of rebel, gangster and street poet," he said in one interview, "and I thought he could be as big as Jimi Hendrix."

In 1972, The Wailers were in England with Danny Sims who had enticed them there with a basic deal with CBS and the plan that they were to tour as the opening act for Johnny Nash (then in the UK charts with his reggae-flavored hit, 'I Can See Clearly Now'). When the tour didn't pan out, and CBS failed to promote the single, 'Reggae On Broadway', one of the trio (most likely

> "Slave driver the table is turned, catch a fire so you can get burned"
>
> **– Bob Marley**

JIMMY CLIFF IN FRONT OF A POSTER FOR THE FILM THAT LAUNCHED HIS CAREER

adding, "he was very surprised that we were civilised people." And no one supported Blackwell's decision to give the group £4,000 (in those days a hefty sum for Jamaican musicians) to take back to Jamaica to record an album—"mother fucking naysayers" he would one day reportedly call them. But Mr Blackwell is a gambler both by inheritance and inclination, and he believed that this small advance (sweetened with the promise of a further £4,000 on delivery), as well as his decision to pay a similar sum, with an override on the next six albums, to buy out the CBS contract, would pay off.

Not surprisingly to those who know just how good a gambler he is, Blackwell's bet on the three Trench Town boys (who he had advised to drop their dated vocal trio concept in favor of a "tight, live band") proved sound. By the end of the year, when the head of Island went back to Jamaica for a visit, he was picked up at his New Kingston hotel by the band, driven to the studio for a listening session, and got to carry back to England what he would end up calling "one of the best albums ever put out".

Catch A Fire, the first concept album in reggae's short and single-driven history, was recorded by the three Wailers in Kingston at Harry J's, Randy's and Dynamic (where the following year the Stones would go to record *Goat's Head Soup*). Still lacking in their ability to play instruments, the threesome were aided by two of the musicians who would themselves one day become Wailers—Aston "Family Man" Barrett on bass, and his brother, Carlton (Carly) on drums. Family Man doesn't remember exactly how much studio time cost in those days, but the album was likely recorded for a steal. Jamaican musicians learned early on to work hard and fast, sometimes cutting several songs in one day.

Robbie Shakespeare, bassist of drum and bass duo Sly & Robbie, speaks affectionately of the days almost 30 years ago when, as a young teenager, he played bass for Bob Marley And The Wailers, on a session that produced two of their best songs: 'Concrete Jungle' and 'Stir It Up'. "Playing on a session in that time come like nuttin'," he says. "But playing on a Wailers session was something." He remembers that on this particular session, "there was great discussion about the intro to 'Concrete Jungle', then when I found a line for the song, Bunny gave me a little part at the front and it all come together." Less time was spent on 'Stir It Up', a simpler song and,

Bob who had just narrowly escaped arrest on a ganja charge) had the idea of checking their countryman, Chris Blackwell, at Island's Notting Hill headquarters. A mutual Jamaican connexion set up a meeting.

Chris Blackwell had been warned that The Wailers were "trouble"—Bunny Wailer remembers Blackwell telling them he'd heard they were "killers and cannibals", for the experienced Kingston session men who played on it, it was an easy couple of hours' work. "In those days," says Robbie, "they would run down (rehearse) a song a long time before putting it on tape." Studio time was, for these ghetto musicians, a valuable commodity, not a minute of which could be wasted.

When it came to paying the musicians, things were also tight. Even when (as in The Wailers' case) an advance on production was paid, the way it was (and is) done in Jamaican music is that the more the budget could be squeezed, the more would be left over for the group. Laughing as he tells the story, Shakespeare says that his session fee per song was then JA$10–$15 (US$11–$16.50 at the time) "but at the end of that day, we nevah get paid."

About a week after leaving The Wailers at Harry J's, Shakespeare went to check Marley at his downtown record shop. "They had a sign outside—it was either Tuff Gong or Intel Diplo (Tosh's label), or maybe it was both—and Bob was leaning on a headpost beside it. We reasoned a while and when it was time to move out, it come money time. Bob gave me some money, but I only got paid for one song—$15.00." But there were no hard feelings. Back in the first bloom of Jamaican pop music, recalls Shakespeare, "it was the norm that if you were doing five songs, the producer would say, 'I can pay for three, beg you for one and owe you for one.' It was like a tight-knit family."

At this point in the conversation, Shakespeare stops in amazement. Throughout the interview, a radio tuned to Power 102, a station not known to present much Marley fare, has been playing in the background. Then, the opening notes of *Catch A Fire*, the intro that Shakespeare has just been talking about are heard. "Rahtid," says Robbie. "See Bob deh". It is one of those intense, goose pimple moments. Even a rude bwoy like Robbie Shakespeare is a little shaken. "I've got chills all down my back." It was February, 1999, in Kingston, but for a second it was 1972 and *Catch A Fire* was still in production.

In the Island Basing Street basement studio known as the Fallout Shelter, the basic tracks were, as Blackwell says, "incredible", but the Island head's additional production gave the album an international pop passport, via overdubs of sounds familiar to rock ears, the guitar licks of Alabama's Wayne Perkins being the most effective.

They called Wayne Perkins the "white Wailer" and today the man who gave 'Concrete Jungle' what Robbie Shakespeare calls "that wicked, wicked solo", ruefully reveals that he never really got credit for his contribution. He is also disappointed that repeated requests for a gold record have been ignored.

Perkins had been working on a second Smith Perkins and Smith album for Island when "Chris stopped me on the spiral staircase going up to the top studio—the main room. He said there was a Wailer project he wanted me to play on. I said, 'Who are The Wailers?'. Chris said, 'They play reggae' and I said, 'That don't help me.'" After a brief rundown on reggae, Blackwell told Perkins, "Just get your Fender, your Les Paul and an amp, and come on down." Says Perkins, "I was a 20-year-old boy from Alabama confronted by these wild-looking Rastas from Jamaica. I had no idea what I was getting into."

It was the first time Perkins had heard reggae— "Desmond Dekker wasn't reggae to me, it was too

> ## "Playing on a session in that time come like nuttin', but playing on a Wailers session was something"
> ### – Robbie Shakespeare

SLY & ROBBIE CIRCA 1984, ARE AS CURRENT TODAY AS IN MARLEY'S TIME

much R&B—and I said, 'Where is my anchor?'". After a bit of fiddling around, Perkins found it, likening reggae to a mix of "the twist and bluegrass, a similar thing to what you can get out of Appalachian or bluegrass". On the third take, with the lights down low, Perkins nailed the solo and "all of a sudden the place went wild". But for Perkins the best part was still to come. "Bob Marley came with this huge spliff and tried (successfully) to stick it in my mouth." Breaking into a hearty Southern laugh, Perkins admits that the rest of the night "went a lot slower".

By the time Bob Marley, Peter Macintosh and Neville Livingston were signed to Island for a total of ten albums, the London label and its founder had earned a reputation for being a savvy and successful marketing agent of rock talent. It was Blackwell's belief that by selling The Wailers to the wider music market in a package it could understand, he could break through reggae's "grass" ceiling and turn the planet on to a world that he, personally, had long been entranced with. In keeping with this strategy, the Island art department designed a novel album sleeve in the shape of a Zippo lighter (all the better to light up your spliff with) that got instant recognition—and rave reviews—from Britain's fickle and very influential music press.

A less gimmicky, but just as eye-catching, sleeve was designed for the second pressing. Featuring a close-up photograph of Bob sporting baby dreads and smoking a giant spliff, taken by Esther Anderson, a woman who was at different times involved with both Marley and Blackwell, this version captured the quintessential Robert Nesta Marley.

STIR IT UP

Said to be Bob Marley's sexiest song and, not surprisingly one of the most popular, the folksy 'Stir It Up' is, in the best Caribbean musical tradition, a masterpiece of *double entendre* and innuendo. Jamaican culture is full of sexual imagery and metaphor, and many of the island's men, especially Rastamen, believe themselves to be Jah's gift to women.

Bob, who had a reputation for being as randy as he was rebellious, admitted that sex (like soccer) was one of his favourite activities, and like many of his peers, likened his sexual prowess to the firm yet yielding strength of trees. 'The Big Bamboo', a long-time humorous favorite of first-time tourists at northcoast hotels sums up this sexual ideal of permanent, if flexible, erection. From this old song came the slang term for penis—"wood"—used to good effect on 'Stir It Up'. The corresponding female term is "pot", allowing for all sorts of interesting plays on words.

Originally written for, and recorded with, Johnny Nash, who included it on his heavily reggae-influenced 1971 hit album, *I Can See Clearly Now*, 'Stir It Up', the second single from the LP, went Top 20 in both the UK (12) and the US (11).

Of the Harry J session that produced The Wailers' version of 'Stir It Up', Robbie Shakespeare says, "Peter, Bunny and Bob came for me." Family Man Barrett, The Wailers' usual bassist was away and Shakespeare, who had played on Bunny Wailer's 'Blackheart Man', and who credits Family Man with teaching him everything he knows about the bass ("he was my angel sent from God"), was called on to play for The Wailers because they liked his sound. (It was because Chris Blackwell liked his sound on 'Concrete Jungle' that he would seek him out a few years later, and eventually sign him and Sly Dunbar to Island).

'Stir It Up' was such a familiar track to The Wailers by the time of the *Catch A Fire* session and is such a basic reggae groove that it was—for a man who has been known to lay down 22 bass lines in one marathon 18-hour session—a very fast lick.

Wayne Perkins remembers it the same way: "'Stir It Up' was pretty easy—Rabbit was on keys and we did the overdubs together. We tried to get the sound as close to each other as we could all through the song, and we did. For the solo, we both used a wah-wah pedal. You can't tell who's playing unless the notes bend and you can't bend keys so that's me." Unlike his clear recollection of how many takes were needed for 'Concrete Jungle', Perkins has no idea what it took for 'Stir It Up'. "'Concrete Jungle' was before the spliff," he grins.

Among the many artists who have covered 'Stir It Up' are Diana King and Judy Mowatt. Mowatt, who originally chose the song because of its sensuality, remarking at the time about Bob's talent for telling a sexual story in subtle terms, declared recently that having switched her allegiance from Selassie I to Jesus Christ, 'Stir It Up' is now against her Christian principles, and that she will therefore no longer perform the song.

> "Bob came with this huge spliff and stuck it in my mouth. The rest of the night went a lot slower..."
> **– Wayne Perkins, guitarist**

SLAVE DRIVER

The haunting legacy of slavery permeates every fiber of Jamaica's being. You can watch it in the walk, hear it in the talk and feel it in the feisty rhythms that blare from every street corner. It is the bottomless well from which almost all of the island's creative expression flows. As the song says, "every time I hear the crack of the whip my blood turns cold".

'Slave Driver' inspired the title of The Wailers' first album, its lyrics telling the slave master that the tables are now turned—"catch a fire, you're gonna get burned".

The song also punctures the myth of freedom—"Today they say that we are free, only to be chained in poverty". Most perceptive is the observation that illiteracy is only a machine to make money. Bad in Marley's days...

three decades later, the poor level of education in Jamaica's school system guarantees that illiteracy—and a plentiful supply of cheap and controllable labor—is in no danger of extinction.

The publishing credit on 'Slave Driver' is given to Bob Marley, as with all of the songs on this album, although, contributions came from all corners, and the mellow, organ-driven musical arrangement of drummer Family Man softens the track's emotional and militant message to such an extent that it infiltrates the mind long before conscious notice is taken of the words.

This plaintive tune also appears on *Rebel Music* and *Songs Of Freedom*. An alternate version appears on the *Talkin' Blues* album.

MIDNIGHT RAVERS

Legend has it that Marley only really came alive after midnight. And, as one story goes, 'Midnight Ravers' was inspired by one of his late-night adventures.

On this particular night, Bob was standing naked in the moonlight (in his garden at 56 Hope Road) eating a piece of roasted breadfruit when he was seduced by a girl named Patricia Williams (who would later bear a Marley son). Early the next morning, so affected was he said to have been by this tryst with Patricia, he wrote the song on the back of the Kingston telephone book.

But though that particular night might have been the original inspiration, there's obviously a wider frame of reference. The lyrics read more like an ode to Kingston's non-stop night life (which, like the songwriter, only "teks life" after 12:00am), and to the singer's non-stop sex life, than to just one night of intense and intimate fun at Hope Road.

"Sexual intercourse is a lovely thing," said the man who viewed his lust for multiple women as his only vice, and describes himself in the closing words of the song as a "night-life raver".

> "Sexual intercourse is a lovely thing"
> – Bob Marley

CONCRETE JUNGLE

Concrete is the antithesis of Rasta sensibility. So is rock guitar to the mindset of most reggae musicians. But when Chris Blackwell brought in Wayne Perkins to add the distinctive rock riffs to the opening bars of *Catch A Fire*, as well as lay down a guitar solo in the break, he not only effected a genre "crossover" before the term was coined, but also captured the edgy mood of the natural Rastaman caught in a concrete maze. Where is the love? Where is the life of those in ghetto captivity? The mind-numbing, sometimes futile struggle for survival offers no frills.

The original architecture of downtown Kingston mixed the formality of Europe with the tropical ease of the Caribbean. The result was the simple but striking wooden and red-brick structures, some of which, although dilapidated, are still standing amid the zinc and concrete that in the past 40 years took over – and separated – the inner city from the rest of Kingston. The music that began to burst out of these concrete prisons was a cry for freedom from the "downpression" that came first from slavery and then was continued by those in power through much more subtle methods. Poverty and illiteracy keeps a man captive as effectively as chains.

Robbie Shakespeare, who with partner Sly, became the bass and the drum anchor of Peter Tosh's backing band, Word, Sound And Power—and who later still, as one of Island Records' most enduring acts, would be the ruling rhythm duo of the island's music scene—played the bass on 'Concrete Jungle', which quickly caught on as yet another of The Wailers' anthems.

On the flip side of the 'Concrete Jungle' single put out by Island Records was a song called 'Reincarnated Souls', which, according to Bunny Wailer, was originally pegged to be the title track of their sophomore album. This album was retitled *Burnin'* after Bunny Wailer "made his stance" against Island plans that clashed with his principles.

'Concrete Jungle' is described by Chris Blackwell as "complex, brilliant". It is a track that has never lost its contemporary and urgent edge.

> A song with an urgent, contemporary edge, 'Concrete Jungle' is described as "complex, brilliant" by Island's Chris Blackwell

PETER TOSH DURING AN EARLY-MORNING PERFORMANCE AT THE WORLD MUSIC FESTIVAL IN MONTEGO BAY IN 1982

ROCK IT BABY

'Rock It Baby' is a classic Bob Marley uptempo love song. Written in the ska style of the day, the banal lyrics (yes, he was capable of banality) are compensated for by the seductive and rollicking role of a ska shuffle stretched in a reggae direction by a "cheng cheng" rhythm guitar. The Wayne Perkins addition of a Santa and Johnnyish steel guitar— "It was a slide guitar with open G tuning," Perkins notes—stretches the track even further from its Kingston roots without breaking the connection. "I wanted to make it different," says Perkins. "I listened to the harmony and the spacing in between for where I could come in." Elaborating further, Perkins says that he "always listens for the counter melody, I either go with it or against it, and if you listen to it you can hear the different changes going by… about six or seven chords in transition. I worked on it for a while, adding a note here and there. With open G

tuning you can do anything… mostly by playing harmony thirds." The end result Perkins describes as "almost Hawaiian… islandish".

Throughout his career, Marley the militant soldier was criticised for his lyrics of lighter mood. Hard yard artistes are supposed to keep their sex and love lives to themselves. The irony in Marley's case is that he started off singing mostly love songs. The really serious stuff came later. Danny Sims, in particular, resisted all Rasta content in his productions, and said that he wanted to break Bob in the States by blending his lovers rock reggae with R&B.

Chris Blackwell, a renegade himself, was the first not only to encourage, but to embrace the singer's rebel side, giving Marley (who believed that truth was synonymous with Rastafari) and the other Wailers free rein to record what they wanted.

NO MORE TROUBLE

Trouble walks everywhere in Jamaica, especially in ghetto enclaves like Trench Town. It is an encouraged culture of badness. Contradicting this tradition, The Wailers' message was one of peace and "livity" instead of war and destruction… and when they spoke, the ghetto was starting to listen. "What is there to benefit from badness?" asked Marley, who often preached that unity was the future and that tribal violence belonged in the past.

'No More Trouble' gets its positive point across with little more than a short, powerful plea and a great hook. That Peter Tosh, a man who courted trouble, arranged it is obvious from the first couple of notes—the interplay of instruments around a trademark Tosh bass line creates a sort of street drama that is often heard in his later work. Marley's soulful vocal injects a soft twist that balances the tension implied by the music, and, as he once avowed was his mission, he "overcomes the Devil with a thing called love".

The ability to straddle opposites is a key element in explaining Marley's far-reaching impact. Unlike Peter Tosh—an equally talented but less influential figure—Bob Marley saw many sides, and once told an interviewer that "man mus' stan' up fi 'im right, an' nah give up 'im right, but me nah gwin fight fi me right" (a belief only tested when he spoke of Africa). Tosh, on the other hand, had no such qualms.

THE POLITICAL AFFILIATION OF THIS AREA OF TRENCH TOWN IS SHOWN BY THE PNP SIGN

KINKY REGGAE

A lot of people say that The Skipper could be kinky, and tales of a hidden darkside are freely told "off the record" by some intimates. By rock standards, however, Marley's kinky indulgences were mild, and, predictably, mostly related to women (with whom he exhibited strong symptoms of a love-hate complex that at times led beyond kinkiness to violence).

The promised intrigue of the lyrics of 'Kinky Reggae'—"brown sugar" was a popular slang term favoured by the original R&B artists (later famously appropriated by The Rolling Stones) meaning sexy brown girl, and "booga wooga", which can be figured out—are not matched by the music itself, which suffers from a fairly pedantic arrangement, and which has no innovative add-ons by outside musicians to liven it up.

Intimates freely tell tales of The Skipper's hidden darkside

BURNIN'

Burnin' and Lootin'

Get Up Stand Up

I Shot The Sheriff

Put It On

Small Axe

Rastaman Chant

Duppy Conqueror

Produced by: Chris Blackwell and Bob Marley

1973

Some of the tracks on *Burnin'* had been recorded at the same time as *Catch A Fire*, but the album was completed at Harry J's Studio in the middle of 1973.

Harry J's, on Kingston's Roosevelt Avenue, is now deserted; its doors locked, and its yard silent. But signs of its illustrious past still linger. A beautifully evocative, eye-level portrait of Bob on the cream courtyard wall bears quiet witness to the scene that was and is no longer. Other portraits of artists that featured in Harry J's past also remain behind, as does a large and colourful painting of a guitar on the trunk of a shady mango tree.

Standing alone in the waning light of a sultry February afternoon, there is an eerie, but not uncomfortable, sense of The Wailers' presence—the echo of the mystical music they made at Harry J's still hanging heavily in the otherwise silent air.

In the beginning, production and arrangement tasks were fairly evenly shared between the three Wailers, but, gradually, Marley took on the responsibility of finishing tracks, as it became clear that the group was not going to survive in its three-man, three-vote format.

Chris Blackwell was in on the mix, just as he had been for *Catch A Fire*—"doubling the length of the songs, over-dubbing, stretching them out like rock songs, and adding instrumental breaks".

On hearing this, manager Don Taylor is adamant that Blackwell brought little to the production end, but others, like engineer Errol Thomson, who was on the board for many of The Wailers' recording and mixing sessions, acknowledge his considerable contribution: "He knows when to bring in this and take out that."

Blackwell is not surprised by Taylor's assertion, but is equally adamant in defending his creative input.

Much of this dispute about Blackwell's right to a producer credit likely stems from the confusion within Jamaica's music industry on what exactly a producer's role is. The common understanding within the trade is that only musicians or engineers produce. The public at large think the "producer" is the executive producer, "the man with the money". The creative producer with an ear is not understood, and that's what Blackwell is. "I think I've got an ear for music, a feel for what good music is." Sly and Robbie go one further: "Chris is a musical prophet."

As to what it was like working with The Wailers in the studio, Blackwell makes mention of how long ago it was—"27 years"—and then says that he worked with all

three only once, "for a very short period in England. It was on *Burnin'*… it was very short, maybe one tune, or two tunes, something like that… I think they were on tour, because they came up to us (from another part of England) for a short time and left."

The tour was for *Catch A Fire*—first the UK and then the United States. But, before the US leg started, Bunny Wailer dropped out and Joe Higgs, The Wailers' first mentor, filled in.

Bunny would re-join the group for an aborted opening slot for the US tour of Sly & The Family Stone (after four shows they were bumped, reportedly for being better than the headliners), as well as the start of the *Burnin'* tour in the UK. This tour, too, was aborted after a show in the British Midlands town of Northampton where, according to tour manager Mick Cater, a flu-stricken Tosh took the onset of thick snow as a sign that "the tour was doomed", which it then became when The Wailers cancelled all remaining dates and boarded a hastily-booked Air Jamaica flight back to Kingston.

The commonly accepted reason behind Bunny's departure from the group is that he didn't want to fly—and it is true that he has a phobia about traveling on the "iron bird". But, Bunny (aka Jah B) tells a different version. "I left because of spiritual reasons… the plans that were made for The Wailers and the direction that The Wailers would be going, I didn't as a Rastaman think I should be going in that direction, so I made a stand on behalf of my other brothers with the intent that they would back me up." But they didn't, and Bunny Wailer decided to back out. "I was just one monkey who don't spoil no show," he muses, sadly.

Sitting outside Mixing Lab Studio on the kind of muggy Kingston morning that can make a New York summer seem cool, the last living Wailer (Peter Tosh was murdered in 1987) is outspoken about his decision to leave The Wailers just when things were getting interesting. "Chris wanted to put us in nightclubs… "freak" clubs. When I asked him why, he said, 'The Wailers are nobody, so we have to play in these places to be somebody.' I said, 'I'm not gonna be

> **"I left The Wailers because of spiritual reasons…"**
> – **Bunny Wailer**

BUNNY WAILER,
THE ONLY SURVIVING
MEMBER OF THE
ORIGINAL BAND

Burnin'—the last album the original three Wailers would record together—would also be the last time the Island head and Tosh would work together. The final break came when Blackwell refused to put out Tosh's solo album because it would have interfered with the marketing plan he had for Marley.

Blackwell's and Bunny Wailer's relationship lasted longer, but the three friends from Trench Town who formed a musical group and called themselves The Wailers were together no longer, and Bob Marley was now Island's sole focus.

Family Man Barrett picks up the story: "Bob said to me, 'What are we going to do now, there's only the three of us left?' So I said, 'Well, the three of us (Bob, Family Man and brother Carly) will just go back on the road.'" Continuing with the air of a man who remembers something as clearly as if it was yesterday, Family Man puts the event into context. "Now, this was also the time that we were supposed to start recording again, and trus' me, *Natty Dread* (as the third Island album would be titled) started off as a dreadful situation. But then Bob said he'd book the time at Harry J's, call in Glaston Anderson on keyboards, Winston Wright on organ, and a couple of horn players, and we just moved on."

In 1975, Marley reminisced about the split and attributed it to a difference in priorities. "Is like dem (Bunny and Peter) don't waan understand dat me cyaan jus' play music for Jamaica alone. Cyaan learn dat way. Me get de mos' learnin' when me travel and talk to other people." He also mentioned that learning was not the only reason he needed to leave the island. "Me affi leave certain times because of politics and politicians wanting favours. Dem love come to you and try get you, and me is a man dat nuh like turn down no man. So me leave Jamaica."

Not surprisingly, his two former bandmates saw it slightly differently. Bunny Wailer, when asked if he blamed Chris Blackwell for the break-up, said "no", going on to say that Blackwell might have had it in mind, because "I saw it in a contract... the first (Island) contract... it stated that The Wailers could be split into different areas and sent as individuals to perform... and that was never the intention of The Wailers."

Pausing for effect, his eyes burning with a tinge of lingering anger, Wailer describes how the group tore up that initial contract, and says, "It was presumptuous,

anybody... bodies are buried... so I just ease off the body plan."

With Bunny gone, it didn't take long for a rift to develop between the strong-willed Peter Tosh and the equally forceful Blackwell (who Tosh liked to call "Whitewell").

"Peter was very difficult," says Blackwell. "Bunny could be, too, but at least if he wasn't going to do something, he'd say so. With Peter, he'd say 'yes', and then not do it."

Marley was more charitable and said of his old friend Tosh's contrariness that "he wanted to have the adventures himself. Him talented enough an' maybe him waan somethin' better dan dis."

telling us in our face that the plans were to split (us)." But, having said this, Bunny Wailer is realistic, and understands that no one could have come between "bredren" who were solidly together, and if all had been well. "In the end, it was up to us," he concludes philosophically. "It was our choice."

Peter Tosh never reached the point of reason where he was able to see it like Bunny Wailer. In a conversation at his house in Kingston, in the same room where just a few days later he would be brutally murdered by six gunmen, Tosh, sitting in a high-backed wicker chair, smoking a Peter Tosh-sized spliff (rolled from a large, plastic bag of ganja that sat at his feet), spoke bitterly about The Wailers' break-up and the years thereafter. "Bob Marley was my student," he said simply, before summing up what happened.

"Once money started to be made and people got famous, everything changed."

Many years after The Wailers went their separate ways, Tosh would be accused of gouging the eyes out of a portrait of his one-time friend and musical partner that hung in the studio at Music Mountain, Jamaica's best recording facility in the Eighties. After he'd cut out the eyes with a penknife, Tosh supposedly turned the painting around so that it would be facing the wall rather than himself, who refused to record with a dead man watching him. Tosh, however, staunchly denied any involvement in this bizarre incident.

As a final note on the dissolution of one of the most gifted trios in the history of pop music, Bunny Wailer stresses the positive, while acknowledging that problems still continue. "With The Wailers solo, you get double, triple, The Wailers' work… it benefited the music, it benefited us as individuals, because we didn't make any money until we split. All the work that we did together as The Wailers, that's still left hanging there, nobody has collected those monies. All the work that we did with Coxsone, Lee Perry, Beverley's, all those monies were pirated, and we've never got anything out of that."

"Nesta", according to Marley's mother, means "messenger", and it was this identity that began to attach itself to Marley as the *Burnin'* album made a word-of-mouth impact on both sides of the Atlantic on its release in 1974. Still relatively unknown in the mainstream music market at the time, The Wailers had acquired an enviable underground reputation which critical praise of *Burnin'* solidified.

The album artwork—photographs once again by Chris Blackwell's girlfriend, Esther Anderson—kept the ghetto feel of *Catch A Fire*, with a black-and-white relief image of the group against a brown board background on the front of the sleeve. Inside is another relief image, this one of Marley smoking a replica of the spliff he sported on the cover of *Catch A Fire*.

Three of the songs on *Burnin'* were not written by Marley. 'One Foundation' was Tosh-penned and performed, and both 'Hallelujah' and 'Pass It On' (stylistically out-of-character tunes for The Wailers) were the work of a now probably wealthy "Jean Watt".

Track for track, *Burnin'* is as good a collection, but not better than *Catch A Fire*. Outstanding cuts like 'Get Up Stand Up', the LP's opening track, and 'I Shot the Sheriff', compare with the previous album's 'Concrete Jungle' and 'No More Trouble'.

In retrospect, however, both releases seem to hover between the sound of The Wailers as they had been, and as they would have become had they not self-destructed.

> ## "Once money started to be made and people got famous, everything changed"
>
> **– Peter Tosh**

A YOUNG PETER TOSH, WHO DESPITE HIS MILITANT IMAGE AND DESERVED REPUTATION FOR BEING DIFFICULT, COULD ALSO BE KIND AND CONSIDERATE.

BURNIN, AND LOOTIN'

"Dat song about burnin' and lootin' is (about) illusions... the illusions of capitalists and dem people with the big bank accounts," said Marley.

To say that 'Burnin' And Lootin'' was controversial in a country where angry, frustrated people routinely block roads with burning tires just to have their voice heard, is far too mild a way to describe the song's actual impact. Jamaica's volatile society has always been very open to the incendiary messages of its musical idols. Although Marley could say a couple of years later that the tune was about "illusions", what it was really about was "burnin', and lootin'" and giving the ghetto youth the go-ahead to help themselves.

Curfews are no longer as common as they were in the Seventies, and when they're enforced, they're usually warranted. But as well as being useful in curbing spontaneous outbreaks of violence, curfews are a clever way to control rebellion. With the growing influence of Rasta and reggae music, rebellion of the self-styled "sufferahs" was but a drum beat away, and the authorities had to find a way to stop it.

"Babylon nuh waan peace, Babylon waan power," was Bob's defence of his militant approach. "My songs have a message of righteousness," he explained. But in another interview, he made it clear that he wasn't a pacifist. "Me don' love fighting, but me don' love wickedness either."

GET UP STAND UP

Used as a unifying anthem by Amnesty International in the era of its big-name candle-light concerts for the cause of human rights, from a political perspective this is Bob Marley's most powerful song. Although the words are more suited to the no-bullshit baritone of Peter Tosh, Bob's soulful wail takes the edge off Peter's stridency and the duet works better than either of their later solo efforts.

In 1975, Marley said of this song, "It say man can live." But by 1978, he was frustrated by its failure to immediately change things. "How long must I protest the same things? I sing 'Get Up Stand Up', and up till now people don't get up." If alive today, he would be desperately frustrated. In the Jamaica of 1999—the people still haven't stood up to an increasingly oppressive and corrupt system. "But dat don' mean dem won'," says Far I, a Trench Town street dread who grew up with Bob. "It jus' tek time."

Ironically, this song, which was one of the last that Peter and Bob would record together, was, says Junior Tucker—who heard the story from Rita Marley, also the catalyst for their one post-split reunion—at a club in London. Bob Marley and the second set of Wailers were appearing live. As Marley began a standard delivery of 'Get Up Stand Up', the audience responded vocally as they always did and, by the second verse, they were on their feet. When the band came out of the second chorus ready to hit the third verse, the lead voice suddenly changed as Peter Tosh, mic in hand, strode on to the stage, shocking Bob as much as the audience. As Tosh's powerful baritone began singing, "We're sick and tired of your isms and schism game," it brought the house down, and a beaming Bob let Peter have the spotlight, skanking beside him in undisguised joy.

At the song's end, Peter turned to a nodding Bob and said, "The Queen feel dat one deh." Then, handing the microphone back to his former bandmate, he left as quickly as he had come.

The two never spoke again.

I SHOT THE SHERIFF

Eric Clapton came across Bob Marley's music quite by accident. As he tells it, he was in the middle of making his critically and commercially successful album, *461 Ocean Boulevard*, at Miami's Criteria Studio when guitarist George Terry played him the *Burnin'* album.

Clapton's cover of 'I Shot The Sheriff' was an almost immediate worldwide hit. Not only did it revitalize Clapton's solo career, but it exposed the work of Bob Marley to a much wider audience. The song's wicked combination of "Wild West" lyrical hook and killer guitar riff cemented it solidly in the minds of the millions who tuned into pop radio in the summer of 1978.

Reflecting on the writing of the song, Marley said, "I wanted to say, 'I shot the police,' but because the (Jamaican) government would have made a fuss, I changed it to 'I shot the sheriff,' instead." Changing the intended target didn't change the meaning, though: "It's the same idea, justice." And the inspiration for the song:

"The elements of that song is people been judging you and you can't stand it no more and you explode, you just explode."

Clapton, unfamiliar with Caribbean ways, asked Marley, after it was recorded, to explain the song. "Him like the kind of music, and him like the melody (but) he didn't know the meaning of the words." Even without the complete understanding he sought, however, Clapton instinctively caught the beat, and came up with a faultless version of what would rival 'Tears In Heaven' as some of his best-known work.

As for whether the original singer resented that someone else made his song a hit, Bob Marley was more than gracious: "We do our own version, but it couldn't be a hit single because the quality wasn't there at the time, and if someone do over a song, maybe they can make it a bit better than the first person who do it."

> "The elements of that song is people been judging you and you can't stand it no more and you explode, you just explode"
>
> **– Bob Marley**

PUT IT ON

A new version of the ska song that marked the marriage celebration of Robert and Rita Marley, this updated rocksteady rendition, like the other old Wailer titles that the group re-did for Island Records, reflected the progress in The Wailers' musical ability, as well as the additional production input of Chris Blackwell after the eight-track tapes were delivered to Island Records.

Blackwell was also the person behind the idea of re-cutting The Wailers' previous work.

"Early on, Bob had problems collecting from these first records because three different people claimed... it's something that's still going on to this day. I'd suggested that the best way to deal with this is just to re-cut the songs... and also, I said, this will mean for every album that we're doing, you already have three or four songs before you even start."

Thus, all of The Wailers' early albums have new licks of old tunes.

The new versions are slightly more sophisticated, and better produced and mixed, but in some cases, not actually better than the originals.

The unison lead vocal of 'Put It On' was mixed with Marley's voice higher in the mix than Bunny's and Peter's, but it's clear that at this point in the recording of the album all three still had significant creative and vocal input.

ERIC CLAPTON – "IT
TOOK ME A WHILE TO
GET INTO IT TO TELL
YOU THE TRUTH,"
HE SAID OF 'I SHOT
THE SHERIFF'

SMALL AXE

Marley's reminder to his Trench Town constituents that all power is not vested in the establishment; the little man has more power than he realizes. So, too, does a little nation. As Jamaicans say, "Wi lickle but wi tallewah" (small but strong).

The lyrics were also said to allude to the big three ("t'ree"), the island's main distributors—Dynamics, Federal and Studio One—and The Wailers' determination to find their own niche in the marketing end of the business, a mission they managed to accomplish. The Jamaican music industry is still ruled by a three-pronged monopoly, but two of the players have changed. Dynamics (owned by soca bandleader, Chinese-Jamaican Byron Lee) now competes with Sonic Sounds (founded by Byron Lee's brother, Neville) and The Wailers' own Tuff Gong.

Originally recorded at Randy's Studio in 1969, 'Small Axe' was the third tune to be re-cut for Island, a move not only good for the group but good for the label's gaffer.

> "Wi lickle but wi tallewah"
> [small but strong]

THE WAILERS' OWN TUFF GONG RECORD SHOP

RASTAMAN CHANT

'Rastaman Chant' is more likely to be heard at a Nyabingi (Rasta retreat) than on a pop music album, but such was the power of The Wailers that they could take what is essentially a religious hymn and make it cool enough for secular consumption.

The percussion pattern on 'Rastaman Chant', played by Bunny Wailer, is the traditional drum beat of Rastafari, the call to arms for Jah children that keeps Nyabingi drummers going through a long night of reasoning and passing of the chillum pipe.

A Nyabingi (the word interpreted by some Rastas as meaning "death to all black and white oppressors", and by others to mean an "irie" gathering) is similar in intent to a religious service, but one which is also an extended (sometimes for several days) social gathering of the island's numerous Rasta clans who take turns hosting the Nyabingi camp. Outsiders are welcome if invited (and after being carefully screened). It is wise to arrive (and leave) accompanied by a respected Rasta bredren, and it is also wise not to try to keep up with the indigenous smokers, some of whom can put away a seven-inch spliff and still carry on an intelligent conversation.

SLY & THE FAMILY
STONE, FOR WHOM
THE WAILERS OPENED
ON FOUR DATES OF A
17-STOP US TOUR
BEFORE BEING FIRED.
THE WAILERS SAID
THEY WERE BUMPED
FOR BEING TOO
GOOD, WHILE SLY
SAID THEY DIDN'T
CONNECT WITH THE
FAMILY AUDIENCE

DUPPY CONQUEROR

Another of the re-cut originals—again with the undeniable input of Chris Blackwell giving the track the sophisticated edge needed for the international market.

Says Blackwell of his marketing strategy: "I wanted to position them as a black group, rather than a reggae act, because reggae acts in general, other than perhaps a Jimmy Cliff, were novelty acts. There was always a reggae hit every year, but it was usually a different

> ## "I dropped the 'Bob Marley' for the first two records so they would have a group image"
>
> **– Chris Blackwell**

artist… it wasn't music that was considered serious musicianship, so I felt that Bob should be presented as a black group—like there was War at that time, or Earth Wind And Fire, or Sly & The Family Stone, black groups which were given a kind of rock sensibility, and I felt that that was what Bob Marley And The Wailers—or really The Wailers, because I dropped the 'Bob Marley' for the first two records so they would have a group image—should be marketed as."

NATTY DREAD

No Woman No Cry

Revolution

Natty Dread

Talkin' Blues

Them Belly Full
(But We Hungry)

Lively Up Yourself

Rebel Music
(3 o'clock Roadblock)

So Jah Sey

Produced by: Chris Blackwell
and The Wailers

THE ORIGINAL NATTY DREAD, HIS NATTY IN ONE OF THE KNITTED TAMS THAT EVERY SELF-RESPECTING RASTAMAN WORE IN THE SEVENTIES

1975

"The *Natty Dread* album is like one step more forward for reggae music. Betta music, betta lyrics… it have a betta feelin'. *Catch A Fire* and *Burnin'* have a good feelin', but *Natty Dread* is improved." So did a satisfied Bob Marley sum up his just-finished *Natty Dread* album in 1974. The third album for Island Records, and the first for Bob as a solo act, it was released to great critical fanfare in February, 1975.

Like its two predecessors, *Natty Dread* was recorded at Harry J's studio. After laying the bed tracks, Family Man remembers that recording was interrupted by an invitation from Taj Mahal to go to California to help mix the *Mo' Roots* album. "Bob accepted and four of us lef'—me, Bob, Alan 'Skill' Cole, and Lee Jaffee. Taj Mahal (one of the first international artists to experiment with reggae) did over 'Slave Driver', too."

While in the United States, Family Man Barrett listened intently to the music on local radio stations, seeking sounds that he could incorporate into The Wailers' music. "I listened to Curtis Mayfield (also a favourite of Marley's), Chaka Khan, JJ Cale… but I especially listened to James Brown, yeah, James Brown's *The Payback*. When I heard that I said to myself, 'This is what we're gonna be doin' on *Natty Dread*.'"

Marley and his Wailers band did the *Natty Dread* overdubs in London, at Island's Basing Street Studio, where American guitarist Al Anderson was recruited, and once again the end result convinced Blackwell to continue backing Bob even though Island had not yet started to recoup the estimated half-million dollars invested. "People read that they're the greatest thing since sliced bread," notes the man who has been critical to the career of many of pop music's better acts, "but they haven't actually got any money coming in. So I would advance royalties to Bob that he hadn't really earned." The key to both bringing in some money, and attracting a wider audience was, Blackwell believed, touring. "Bob's success came from people seeing him and saying, 'Fuck, I can't believe this guy,' and then going and buying the record." Bob Marley, however, was not an easy man to get back on the road after the early tours turned sour. In fact, some of the executives at Island were getting a little edgy. It was at this critical juncture that Don Taylor began to manage the rising reggae star.

"One good thing I have to say about Don Taylor," says Chris Blackwell—about a man who has very little good to say about him—"He was able to get Bob on the road."

Taylor for once, agrees with Blackwell's version of events. "Yes, it was definitely me who got him to go out on tour."

Don Taylor, like Bob grew up on the streets of downtown Kingston and, in his words, began hustling at a very young age. He perfected his technique, he confides, on easily-conned cruise ship passengers (a hustling tradition still practised today).

"I was," he says, "all things to all persons… tour guide, pimp or hustler." His transition from working the streets to working behind the scenes in the entertainment business happened when Taylor, who had been providing a personal valet service to visiting R&B singers, accepted Jerry Butler's offer to join his tour as his valet, a break from which he parlayed into an extended stint as manager of black acts like Little Anthony and The Imperials.

Taylor's street skills served him well in the tricky, tough and Mob-riddled world of American music that he was now part of. By the time he approached Bob Marley with his offer to manage him, Taylor had paid his dues and knew what he was doing. Marley, sensing that Taylor had considerably more "smarts" than anyone else within Kingston's thriving but unsophisticated music world, agreed that Taylor could join his team.

One of the first things Taylor did was renegotiate The Wailers' contract with Island. Having quickly realized that the existing agreement had been nullified with the departure of two of the three signatories, and he considered that a new one signed by Bob Marley was also of dubious legal standing, Taylor used the situation to his advantage, raising the bottom line from what Jamaicans call "sweetie money" to a decent deal, which included the bargain $250,000 purchase of Blackwell's 56 Hope Road house where Bob had already been living for a couple of years, and which nowadays houses a rudimentary "museum" which showcases an unimaginative display of Marley mementoes. It also houses an Elektra Records-financed SSL board update of Marley's original studio (used mainly by his children).

The new contract was, signed says Taylor, not by

> "I was all things to all persons… tour guide, pimp or hustler"
> — **Don Taylor, manager**

Bob Marley And The Wailers but by himself, and contained an unique clause for the "provision and supply of marijuana". This rider would frequently prove difficult to honour when Bob Marley And The Wailers toured beyond ganja-friendly territory.

But Taylor's most immediate job as manager was to organize the *Natty Dread* tour. He also, he says, endorsed and continued what Bob Marley had begun on *Natty Dread*, the registration of previously unrecorded Marley-penned songs in other names (like Carlton and Aston Barrett, Vincent Ford and R Marley—which could be either Robert or Rita) to avoid the publishing rights of Cayman Music—a company owned jointly by Danny Sims and Paul Castellano, reported to be the don of the notorious Gambini family. This rather devious practice, although initially controllable via blanket royalty collection by the artist's British Virgin Islands' company, Bob Marley Music, would later prove problematic when some of those credited would swear that they had come by the credits legitimately, begging the question of why, if Marley was indeed the sole writer, pseudonyms weren't used instead.

It was about this time that keyboardist Tyrone Downie was brought into The Wailers by Family Man Barrett. Downie, in his early teens at the time, says that he "was a Wailers' groupie… in love with revolution" and modestly denies that he contributed very much to the band's music, insisting that "instead of contributing, I was just sucking it all up". An on-again, off-again Rasta—he "had locks three times"—Downie, now a "bald-head" and living in Paris, believed wholeheartedly in Marley's cause and, despite his denial of being an integral part of The Wailers' creative process, has many fans within the Jamaican music industry who would argue otherwise. But Tyrone Downie is stubborn in his humility, and not a little cautious in what he says these days and to whom he says it.

> ## "It was the Barrett brothers who gave Bob a paper to write on"
> **– Tyrone Downie**

"If anybody deserves credit," Downie argues, "it is Family Man," later saying that "it was the Barrett brothers who gave Bob a paper to write on".

Family Man Barrett claims it was he who first set up The Wailers' signature female harmony sound, which started, he says, during the recording of *Natty Dread* with the two sisters of a friend in London who "used to find us herb," and ended with the I'Threes, who came in when recording was finished and learned the harmony parts for the live tour. Family Man no longer remembers the names of the two sisters, but says that he intends to look them up soon, "so that they can get proper credit for their work".

The I'Threes—Rita Marley, Judy Mowatt and Marcia Griffiths—would take over the harmony next and would become Marley's permanent backing trio. They were also solo singers in their own right, with Griffiths getting the nod for having the strongest vocal cords. "It was Marcia's voice that we relied on the most," says Family Man. "We would doubletrack her and then ping-pong the tracks together, adding Rita and Judy to that," says the musician, who is generally credited with most of the band's musical arrangements.

Marcia Griffiths, already a very successful reggae singer when she joined the I'Threes, started out singing at Duke Reid's Treasure Isle, another of the island's seminal labels. When Treasure Isle was sold to Sonia Pottinger—a rare female producer in an industry so sexist that it still calls itself a "fraternity". Griffiths, dissatisfied with the money she was getting from Pottinger, moved on (with engineer Errol Browne, who would later become one of The Wailers' main engineers, and today is still with Tuff Gong), to Studio One. Judy Mowatt—who has now renounced Rastafari to revert to Christianity—began her career in the late-Sixties as the third member of a female group, called the Gaylettes, but had also gone solo by the time she linked with her I'Three "sistren", and with Bob's best friend, footballer Skill Cole, the father of three of her children.

The first Wailers' song that the I'Threes sang on was 'Jah Live', and Mowatt contradicts Family Man by saying that the trio did sing on *Natty Dread*. But all agree that the I'Threes were there when Bob Marley And The Wailers hit Toronto, the first stop on their North American *Natty Dread* tour.

Michael Cohl, then a small local promoter who, by the Nineties had (via brilliant business deals with acts like The Rolling Stones) become the biggest in North America, had booked The Wailers into Massey Hall, a traditional, turn-of-the-century music hall with great acoustics and a 2,000-seat capacity. The show was a stunning, sold-out success, and Don Taylor was both relieved and jubilant that the show—in a city known in the business as an accurate harbinger for the rest of the continent—had come off so well. "I knew then," he says, "that a superstar was born." *Rolling Stone* magazine sensed it, too, giving Marley a late-summer cover captioned, "Rastaman with a Bullet".

Later that same year, Island Records released the *Live!* album, produced by Steve Smith and for which Island, Taylor claims, paid US$500,000, reportedly because the live collection was not accepted by Chris Blackwell as part of The Wailers' ten-album deal.

Live! contained only seven songs—a meagre offering by today's standards, but including some outstanding cuts, like 'I Shot The Sheriff' and 'No Woman No Cry'— taken from several concerts, including the two legendary gigs Marley played at London's Lyceum on July 19 and 20, 1975, with Third World opening. The UK's *Melody Maker* gushed over The Wailers' four sold-out shows (as well as the two London concerts they also played Birmingham and Manchester). "The Wailers Conquered Britain" was the headline.

Meanwhile, back in Jamaica, Michael Manley's tropical honeymoon was already coming to a crashing end. The man that had so mesmerized the masses in 1972 had since found that sweet words alone couldn't run a country, and that as effective an election tool as his highly symbolic "rod of correction" (his ever-present stick that he had been entrusted with by Emperor Haile Selassie some years before) had been, speaking stirringly and carrying a big stick was no substitute for action.

The dismal economic reality of the Jamaican poor, tabled in Parliament by the Prime Minister himself the preceding year—that 30-odd thousand people were making less than $10 a week, 60,000 earning less than $15, and 100,000 taking home less than $20—showed no sign of changing. None of this would prevent his re-election in 1976, giving rise to a new truism: that in Jamaica, history doesn't just repeat itself, it becomes a tradition, thus ensuring that this island of so much potential never moves forward.

Preferring to be seen as apolitical (and sometimes insisting that he be depicted in this way), Marley nonetheless kept consistent company with influential insiders from both parties. In large part, this was to ensure that his music got airplay, and it was a

JAMES BROWN'S THE PAYBACK WAS THE INSPIRATION FOR MUCH OF THE MUSICAL ARRANGEMENT ON NATTY DREAD, ACCORDING TO FAMILY MAN BARRETT

concession he would live to regret. In the Seventies, payola was political, and didn't require the paying over of money (at least not to the radio stations). Political strong-arm tactics were the most frequent and potent means to an end that included maximum spins by the leading radio jocks of the day.

Were Marley here today, it wouldn't be as simple as hanging out with the right people. Cash has replaced political connections and no one gets through the music system without depositing large quantities of it in the hands that can open the tightly-monitored doors to public exposure. Distribution, radio play, media coverage, concert bookings, video airings and chart listings are all, to varying degrees, controlled by a small, but very powerful, group.

THE I'THREES, JUDY
MOWATT, RITA
MARLEY AND MARCIA
GRIFFITHS, WENT ON
TO RECORD AS A
DISTINCT GROUP,
WEARING MORE
ORNAMENTAL STAGE
GEAR THAN THEY DID
WITH BOB

NO WOMAN NO CRY

One of Marley's most popular and poignant songs, 'No Woman No Cry' was written about his days in the cramped concrete house he shared with his mother at 19 Second St—"the government yard in Trench Town". Its appeal lies in its truth—there really was a Georgie who "kept a logwood fire burnin' through the night" on which he and Marley would cook their morning cornmeal porridge, a habit that, like his Trench Town roots, he would never outgrow.

The writer's credit on the song is given to Vincent Ford (aka "Tartar"), a "bredren" from downtown days who, popular belief has it, now lives poor, disabled, and almost forgotten, in a small shack behind the Bob Marley Museum, but who, in other versions has recently collected healthy royalties and is doing OK. Family Man says that Tartar contributed to the song but didn't write it, and others close to the scene concur. Don Taylor, however, sticks with the story that the credit was given to Tartar (who also got a credit on 'Crazy Baldhead', 'Roots, Rock, Reggae' and 'Positive Vibration') for financial convenience only.

'No Woman No Cry' was released as a single in Great Britain and stayed in the charts for seven weeks, rising at one point to Number 20. Remarkably, in 1981, shortly after Marley's demise, it re-entered that same chart, this time peaking at Number 8.

The superb live version of the song (that appears on

Live!) was recorded at The Roxy in LA. It comes up in conversation with Chris Blackwell when he is asked what his most memorable moment with Bob was. "There were so many," he answers, "but I'll give you one." He looks straight ahead at the still, sapphire green sea that fronts his "*GoldenEye*" property. "It was at The Roxy. It was the first time I heard the audience sing along with 'NWNC', and I thought, 'if we could get a live record with the audience singing along'—it had such an incredible atmosphere. That's when I decided to put out a live album."

> "Me really love 'No Woman No Cry' because it means so much to me. So much feeling me get from it. Really love it"
>
> **– Bob Marley**

REVOLUTION

On April 14, 1999, the PNP finance minister, Omar Davies, announced in the budget, a whopping 31 per cent increase in the price of gasoline (which translated at the pumps to about US$1.00 jump per gallon). There was, he said, no alternative. Over the following few days, the country is crippled by hundreds of random roadblocks. "Nation Ablaze" is the theme of CVM Television's nightly news as fires burn everywhere. Crudely-made cardboard picket signs saying PJ (Prime Minister Patterson) must go", "The people cyaan tek no more", and "Revolution is a must" are waved from every street corner, and for the first time in the nation's history, the middle classes are out in full support of the poor.

Twenty-five years after 'Revolution was released, its relevance is stronger than ever. Bob Marley is, once again (in Stevie Wonder's words) "hot on the box", and this persuasive call to arms is one of the favoured songs of the day, another being the contrasting universal plea for peace, 'One Love'.

After three days of chaos, the riots end with the government's pledge to "roll back" the gas tax 50 per cent, a move that stops the violence, but is greeted with scepticism by many who question Patterson's ability to perform the function of prime minister and who now rate him as Jamaica's most unpopular head of government ever.

In 1974, Marley's reference to revolution was of far different origin. Michael Manley's Democratic Socialist government was intent on forging an alliance with Fidel Castro's communist Cuba, and, initially, the poor of Jamaica thought this to be a good thing, worthy of a revolution. After a short time in office Manley's credibility was eroding even among his core supporters. Joshua (his Biblical nickname) was seen to have flaws and Marley, who had once courted politicians on both sides, began to distance himself from the system. 'Revolution' was his first open reference to his disillusionment. "Never make a politician grant you a favour, they will want to control you for ever," was a warning gleaned from personal experience.

MARLEY ARRIVES FOR A 1974 SHOW AT THE BIRMINGHAM ODEON ON THE NATTY DREAD TOUR

NATTY DREAD

ZIGGY MARLEY DIDN'T
START 'LOCKING' UNTIL
HE LEFT ARDENNE
HIGH SCHOOL

This was first released as 'Knotty Dread', as dread-locksed youths were first known ("natty" came into the language from the Jamaican pronunciation of "knotty").

Initially, the popularity of dreadlocks seemed synonymous with the increase in the popularity of the hair-style's most influential wearer. As Marley told Third World's Ibo Cooper when he came back from an early tour, "The whole a Jamaica full a Bob Marleys." But the sudden spread of locks didn't make them any more socially acceptable. Those of Marley's children who had sported locks (like Ziggy) were forced to trim before being accepted at the strict uptown schools they attended in the Eighties. It was not until they were out of school and independent that they could dread.

In the Nineties, school rules have relaxed greatly and most schools now allow the dreadlocksed children of Rastas to attend as long as their locks are contained by caps. But discrimination against "natties" still exists. Unless famous or wealthy, those who "locks" are still perceived as socially inferior by the uptown "verandah set", a perception not helped by the fact that the island's street population of "mad men" are (solely by reason of not cutting their hair) naturally natty, nor by the reality that many who dread are, in the Jamaican parlance, more "rascal" than Rasta.

TALKIN' BLUES

The rebel with many causes said that the line was not to be taken literally, but the violent sentiment expressed by Marley in 'Talkin' Blues'—"I feel like burning a church now"—continues to draw criticism. If Bob Marley was indeed a man of peace, the question is asked, how could he sing of bombs (or even of revolution)? But the very complex character that was Bob Marley answered this himself: "I don't come down on you really with blood and fire, earthquake and lightning, but you must know seh that within me all a that exists." And 'Talkin' Blues' is one of the best

examples of how Marley's music always tempered the tart message with a sweet melody.

'Talkin' Blues' (though credited solely to Carlton Family Man Barrett) probably had its origins in Marley's brief association with his father. Recounting that Mr Marley Sr habitually spoke of "stones for my pillow and the sky is my roof" (during what she describes as his "frequent weepy moods"), Cedella Booker believes that her son's "cold ground was my bed last night, rock stone was my pillow", spoken of in 'Talkin' Blues' came directly from his father's frequent lament.

THEM BELLY FULL (But we hungry)

The original Island tracksheet for 'Them Belly Full (But We Hungry)' illustrates the increasing musical complexity of The Wailers' music—from 2-track to 16 and now, on this album, to 24 (although most of the songs recorded still didn't exceed the familiar 16).

An interesting engineer's note at the bottom of the tracksheet says, "Track (1) is duff", and cautions, "transfer track 2nd (2) numbers before any O/D, or check 24T card".

Al Anderson overdubbed two lead guitar tracks on this song, and tracks 10 and 22 had tenor sax (despite Chris Blackwell's belief that Bob's music was better off without horns—"I just didn't like it," he says, pointing out that if nothing else it created a logistical problem on tour—"more plane tickets, more hotel rooms"—and also noting that The Wailers had never worked out a place for the horns onstage).

Of the lyrics, Marley said in an interview, "Your belly's full, but we're hungry for the love of our brethren. Food might be in your belly, but there's more to living than just filling it. Where's the love of your brother?" Or, as Family Man puts it, the song is about "trying to feed the multitude with just a handful of corn".

During the 1999 riots, the song's perennial relevance would hit home again. "The people are hungry," said JLP Member of Parliament, Babsy Grange, letting her large audience at a women's peace rally (called to end the turmoil) finish off the thought themselves… "and a hungry man is an angry man".

LIVELY UP YOURSELF

Written as 'Liven Up Yourself' on the original Island track-sheet (perhaps a grammatical correction of the Jamaican vernacular), this song ventured over the familiar 16-track line to 18, but then Track 17, a second backing vocals track, was crossed out. An engineer's note on Track 1 (organ) reads, "keep low", and, as on 'Them Belly Full', two extra guitar tracks have been overdubbed by Al Anderson.

It is one of Marley's "irie vibes" songs, frequently dropped in by the artist, says former Marley art director Neville Garrick, "to get the crowd moving during stageshows" (a ploy Prince would copy with his cover of the song in the mid-Eighties). "They would drop it in," Garrick says, "and send Junior Marvin (often called the 'second star' by the press)out there."

'Lively Up Yourself' is still a crowd-pleaser when covered, as it often is, by other reggae bands. A paean to the power of reggae music and its ability to lift the most oppressed of spirits, and "soothe (the warring instincts of) the savage beast", 'Lively Up Yourself' is another Wailers' song pulled back into public consciousness in the tense days that follow the April, 1999 rioting.

> "Soothe (the warring instincts) of the savage beast"
> **– Bob Marley**

REBEL MUSIC

Throughout the Seventies and Eighties, police and Army roadblocks were commonplace. To be stopped by soldiers in full military garb, and to be harassed for no reason, was almost a certainty, especially when driving from town to town. 'Rebel Music' was based on a real roadblock encountered by Marley while driving across the island with his then girlfriend, Esther Anderson, a one-time love interest of Chris Blackwell's, and the photographer responsible for the covers of both *Catch A Fire* and *Burnin'*.

Called 'Roadblock' more often than by its correct title, this song is Don Taylor's favourite, because, he says, it tells a story not just of a roadblock, but of the ghetto child's life: there is always something trying to block you.

Whether it was the people who took the roadblock idea from the police or vice versa, the blocking of roads by the island's citizens is now a well-entrenched Jamaican tradition (dating back at least to the Sixties, and, some old-time Jamaicans say, the Forties).

Roadblocks are the people's way of dealing with any real or perceived injustice and too often the only way the government pays any attention to its constituents' complaints. Using anything at hand—tires, trees, rocks, car wrecks and cast-off appliances (which are all set on fire), roadblocks can create havoc, and not infrequently create additional income for the perpetrators who will allow safe passage in exchange for a "pass" fee.

> Roadblocks are the people's way of dealing with any real or perceived injustice and too often the only way that the government pays any attention

BOB MARLEY
LIVE IN 1980

SO JAH SEY

Officially credited to Will Francisco and Rita Anderson (Marley), 'So Jah Sey' is another of the songs that Don Taylor says he "picked (writers') names at random" for, but the tune bears Marley's unmistakable lyrical cadence and content—a combination of Biblical phrase, Jamaican proverb, patois color and pop hooks.

Neither Rita, nor any of Marley's "seeds" will ever have to sit "in the sidewalk and beg bread", as he states in the song, since five of his 11 offspring (legitimate and otherwise) got a million dollar settlement from his estate and the rest remain as beneficiaries. Prior to this point, though, says Don Taylor among others, some of the Gong's illegitimate children went without support for several years. "If my only crime was to make Rita accountable to the outside children, then I'm happy I did it," says Taylor, answering a question about the negative way many in the Marley camp perceive him. "I said it was unfair that these children weren't getting funds—some of them were only getting JA$80.00 (then about US$20.00) a week—and I was called in to expose this by Mrs Booker (who had adopted Rohan, one of the illegitimate heirs)."

Only three of Bob's children were borne by Rita. The others—Rohan, Julian, Robbie, Kymani, Karen, Damian, and Makada—came courtesy of a total of seven "baby mothers". Also acknowledged as an heir to the estate was Stephanie, Rita Marley's daughter by a man named Ital.

ZIGGY MARLEY WITH HIS SISTERS— CEDELLA FAR RIGHT AND SHARON AT THE BACK, REACHING FOR THE BABY

RASTAMAN VIBRATION

BOB MARLEY IN HAPPY MOOD, GLOUCESTER ROAD, LONDON, 1978

War

Johnny Was

Crazy Baldhead

Positive Vibration

Rat Race

Night Shift

Who The Cap Fit

Cry To Me

Roots, Rock Reggae

Smile Jamaica

Produced by: Bob Marley And The Wailers

1976

An album that was, according to Chris Blackwell, "a conscious attempt to break into the black American market", *Rastaman Vibration* was released in a year of political chaos on Jamaica that, from Marley's perspective, began with the death of a stepfather he had grown to love, and ended with a botched attempt—by an estimated seven gunmen—on his own life. Two days after that, he appeared at a free concert for the people—Smile Jamaica—in downtown Kingston.

Bob Marley, whose idea it had been to do the benefit show, did not want Smile Jamaica to be politicized, but Michael Manley had other plans. A couple of days after the prime minister had approved the concept, and Marley had announced the show at a press conference, Manley had his own press conference to announce the date of the next election, timed to closely follow the Smile Jamaica concert. Bob Marley was angered by Manley's crafty political move, but chose neither to cancel nor postpone the free show for the people. Then came the shoot-out at his Hope Road home.

Speculation about whether or not Marley would brave the stage at the Smile Jamaica event (which would become one of the two milestone local concerts of his career) ended when the red vehicle that had carried him, under armed guard, from his Blue Mountain hideaway, pulled up backstage. The still-bandaged singer took the mic, and after hugging a beaming Michael Manley, addressed an emotionally explosive audience of about 50,000 people with the stirring and appropriate words of 'War'.

Like all election years in Jamrock, 1976 was marked by the kind of senseless violence that serves, on this very controlled island, only to maintain the political status quo. On June 19, the Governor General, or "GG", Sir Florizel Glasspole, declared a State of Emergency to combat what incumbent Prime Minister Michael Manley saw as a joint plot by opposition leader Edward Seaga, and the United States' CIA, to discredit his party. In the middle of all this, Bob Marley was being increasingly seen as supporting Manley's People's National Party (PNP), a suspected allegiance which many feel was the reason he almost died on the night of December 3, when two carloads of gunmen got into the grounds of 56 Hope Road, and shot the singer, wife Rita, and manager Don Taylor, who took five of the bullets meant for Bob, and whose legs, crossed as he sits on the cream-coloured couch in his living room, a mere stone's throw from where he was shot, still bear the jagged scars of that night.

As it was later told, Marley had just taken a rehearsal break and was eating a grapefruit when the first shot was fired. Taylor crossed the room in the line of fire, sparing Marley all but one of the shots intended for him. Rita Marley was hit in the head when she stepped out from her yellow Volkswagen to investigate the noise that everyone initially thought had come from fireworks, while The Wailers, so the story goes, took shelter in the bathtub.

Nancy Burke, a friend of both Cindy Breakespeare and Marley, was on her way to Hope Road and heard the shots as she approached the property. Turning into the gates, minutes after the gunmen had fled, she describes the scene as ominous. "There was total silence," she says. "I thought everyone had been massacred."

The injured trio were quickly taken north up Hope Road to the University Hospital, following which Marley, released as soon as his minor wound was dressed, was moved up the adjacent mountain to Chris Blackwell's isolated Strawberry Hill estate in Irish Town. Marley later said, "Them come through the door and start shoot, blood claat. Dat mean me cyaan move. One time I move to one side, and the gun shot flew over deh… the feelin' I had was to run hard but God jus' move mi in time. His Majesty was directing me and as me move me feel like I get high… I tell yuh, Rasta dangerous."

Third World, the opening act on Smile Jamaica, decided, despite understandable misgivings, to do the show as scheduled. Ibo Cooper, the group's keyboardist, remembers that Marley called him at home "every five minutes" for Cooper to confirm that he was leaving his house for the venue. "He would not rest until I said I was leaving my yard." When Third World started to play before a "peaceful but excited" crowd, it was obvious, says Cooper, "that the people wanted Bob". Given a radio by the show's producer and asked to call Marley, Cooper says that "only then did Bob finally decide to come".

Cat Coore remembers a friend of his who was with Bob telling him that Marley, accompanied by a heavy

> ## "Rastaman vibration gonna cover the earth like the water cover the sea"
>
> **– Bob Marley**

police escort, came down Gordon Town Road (a very narrow and dangerous mountain road) at full speed, arriving at the venue just as Third World's set finished.

Some of The Wailers decided not to play. "Some of Third World stood in for them," recalls Cooper, "but then, as the music took over, one by one The Wailers started to come onstage, pick up a bass, or a guitar and begin to play". The set continued with a mix of musicians from both bands. "The song list was spontaneous," Cooper says. "Bob would call each song in the middle of the song before it, and every song somehow fit together... it was like he was telling a story, chapter by chapter." As for the singer, "he was in another world, transported somewhere far beyond the stage", delivering his militant message in his usual peaceful and mesmerising style. After the show, the huge crowd surprised the cynics by dispersing quietly. As Cooper puts it: "like a breeze blew them away".

"Smile Jamaica sealed the election, says Cat Coore.

Rastaman Vibration was the perfect release for this tumultuous year. It was an album that reflected Marley's growing belief in the peaceful philosophy of Rastafarianism and his new alliance with the Twelve Tribes of Israel (the likely result of the many nights spent "reasoning" with the elders in Rasta-dominated Bull Bay). Sporting a burlap-like sleeve, designed by Neville Garrick after The Skipper, pointing to a piece of burlap which had a photo leaning against it, said "album design

> "His Majesty was directing me and as me move me feel like I get high... I tell yuh, Rasta dangerous"
>
> **– Bob Marley**

dat", and which the liner notes suggested could double as a cutting board for cleaning herb, went immediately into the Top 10 in Britain and was an even bigger seller in the US, where it peaked at Number 8, proving that the minstrel from the Tribe of Judah's had delivered a hip message for the times.

The December election result surprised no one. As Bob Marley was the musician for those troubled times, Manley was the politician with the power to pull the people behind him as no other before him. Not even his father, the revered Norman Manley, founder of the party his son had just led to his second victory, could come close to the reverence accorded to Michael.

Tall, elegant of manner, but able to touch the people on such a visceral level that the Promised Land was not only a viable possibility, but with "Joshua" leading them, a distinct probability. With his "rod of correction"—a stick said to have been a personal gift from Selassie I—held high, Michael's authority was absolute, and the people were wild with hope for a future in which they would have a say. All of this despite a first four-year term in office that had been a frightening failure.

With a commitment to the citizens of Jamaica that he would never, ever begin to fulfill, Manley's reign began with the belief that Jamaica was at long last coming into its own, and continued in 1976 with the fallacy that it was just taking a little longer. Middle-class sceptics saw the situation a little more clearly, and the flights out of Jamaica continued, filled with disillusioned emigrants.

Marley's departure from his home a few months earlier, shaken and very grateful to be alive, had a profound effect on his work. As Errol Browne says: "After the shooting, his lyrics got more serious."

WAR

Putting the powerful words of Emperor Haile Selassie, King of Kings, Conquering Lion of the Tribe of Judah, to music was Marley intimate Alan "Skill" Cole's idea. Originally delivered to the United Nations in 1968, Selassie's passionate plea for human rights acquires additional power when poetically edited by Marley, and accompanied by the insistent drive of drum and bass. Although he wasn't given a writer's credit, Selassie's spirit lives on in this song, for who among those familiar with the opening bars can ever ignore the truth in the words —"Until the philosophy which holds one race superior... and another... inferior... is finally... and permanently...

discredited… and abandoned. Everywhere is war."

War was on everyone's lips in the Jamaica of the mid-Seventies. With tourism at an all-time low (middle America, and even the more adventurous Europeans scared away by the escalating violence), and the guns that were normally confined (safely) to the ghetto finding their way into more and more uptown areas, the middle classes of Jamaica were fleeing by the hundreds. Manley, who saw this mass migration as being akin to treason, encouraged the exodus, telling the unfaithful departing to hurry "get their seat" on one of the numerous daily flights to Miami.

JOHNNY WAS

Popularly believed to be about Carlton "Batman" Wilson, brother of singer Dellrow Wilson, it is much more likely that the lyrics of 'Johnny Was' pay tribute to the thousands of ghetto "yout'" shot down by "stray" bullets on the divided Kingston streets over the past 40 years, and the mothers who have cried so much that they are said to have no more tears left to shed.

Ironically, Marley's own mother would cry when a bullet struck her son, who, unlike so many of his Trench Town peers, would, by surviving the attack, give her equal reason to "express great joy", she says.

The bullet that struck Marley wasn't a "stray"; it was meant for him. But it did come from the same guns of political rivalry that have split Kingston's inner-city communities since the red, white and blue Union Jack was replaced by the green, gold and black flag of independent Jamaica when Britain pulled out in 1962. Marley, many believe, was a growing threat to the two-party political divide. His popularity with people of both the orange (PNP) and green (JLP) persuasion was being increasingly perceived as forming a bridge to a unity that would not be in the best interests of a system that depends on its warring political tribes for survival.

Though it was commonly accepted that politics

prompted the shooting, and that the CIA was somehow involved, no one was apprehended. Marley said in an interview that he knew who his attackers were, but declined to name them. Don Taylor insists that "the catalyst was the CIA", and says that Manley told him that the CIA wanted to overthrow him. But, Taylor adds, the JLP played a major role, too, going on to relate that the actual gumen were later executed after trial by a ghetto court.

EMPEROR HAILE SELASSIE I OF ETHIOPIA, KING OF KINGS

AL ANDERSON IN DECEMBER 1978· HE PLAYED LEAD GUITAR FOR PETER TOSH AND MARLEY

CRAZY BALDHEAD

"Baldhead" is Jamaican slang for anyone with closely-trimmed hair, the "suits" of government and business who opposed the rebellious and initially somewhat scary stance of Rastafarianism, which visibly proclaimed its anti-social philosophy by the throwing away of colonial hair combs, and the uninhibited growth of dreadlocks. The social stigma of long, natural (though some were painstakingly trained) locks lasted long past the days of Bob Marley. It was not until the Nineties that dread-locked students were allowed into Jamaican schools. Prisons also enforced the "no dreadlocks" rule until very recently, and shaved the locks off the heads of all inmates before mug shots were taken.

Locks nowadays are often tied under multi-coloured, tight turbans as the "bobo" dreads, a radical interpretation of the original Rastafarian order grow in number and threaten the dominance of the "natty dread". The locksmen that ruled in Bob's day are now greying, and no longer nearly as menacing to the establishment as they seemed. But one thing hasn't changed and that is the hold that the baldhead has on Babylon. Despite Marley's fervent wish, no one, yet, has been able to "chase those crazy baldheads out of this town".

'Crazy Baldhead' boasts one of the most emotive vocals of Marley's career. The depth of his passion for Rastafari echoes in every word, and the political importance of the sentiments expressed are underscored dramatically by Al Anderson on lead guitar.

POSITIVE VIBRATION

If there is one phrase that captures the mood of those early days of Rasta, "positive vibration" is it, for despite the propaganda of those who stood to gain by undermining the movement, Rastafari was never violent, never evil, and certainly never anything to fear. It did oppose the system, and it did promote change in the way things had always been done, but the main tenets of the reggae revolution were peace and love, and irie and positive vibrations. As Bob explained it: "Positive vibrations… that's reggae music."

All reggae concerts in the Seventies, and even some in the early Eighties—whether the featured act was Bob Marley, Bunny Wailer, Third World, Burning Spear, or the ever-controversial, outspoken Peter Tosh—came with a guarantee of a "positive and upful", never-to-be-forgotten experience (and it wasn't just the ganja). In stark contrast to the post-Marley years when the discordance of dancehall music erupted and then took over, and ganja was replaced by cocaine, and war promoted over peace, the rebellious content of reggae's early lyrics came wrapped in such innocent melodies that the hordes of red, green and gold-festooned fans would have happily skanked all the way to the revolution.

"'Cause it's a new day, new time, new feeling, yeah! Positive I and I vibrations, yeah," sang Marley, and everyone wanted to believe him. Amid the carnage left behind by the election was the growing hope (yet to be realized) of a better future. Bob Marley's songs especially had "struck a chord with the kids", Ibo Cooper says, "and the youths were eager to build a new Jamaica. What Bob was saying was the right thing for the times."

RAT RACE

'Rat Race' was a timely song of both social and political significance. In it, Marley not only distances himself—and Rasta—from the CIA, letting the US intelligence agency (which he correctly suspected was monitoring him) know that Rasta wants no part of it, but also, on another level, warns against social complacency. According to classified CIA documents (declassified after his death), Bob Marley, described as the "reggae star", was indeed being watched. The shooting of Marley ("probably political") was reported as an event that, regardless of cause, "will be with us for some time given (his) popularity". The report also noted that "contributing to this view is the fact that while the newspapers have given the shooting prominent coverage, the reporting has been curiously uninformative".

The CIA interest in Marley would later lead to speculation of possible involvement in his death, that, along with other conspiracy theories, still linger today.

The social message of the song was directed at the complacent "MCJs" (middle-class Jamaicans), and warned that the perceived "peace and safety" of their affluent St Andrew suburbs were in danger of "sudden destruction". Also, the "collective security" of hiding behind burglar bars (a reality of life on the island) was neither safe nor permanent… everyone, whether "gorgon" (leader), or "hooligan", shared the same destiny.

On a more mundane note, Marley never forgot the rat race of the Chrysler assembly line where he worked when he went to Wilmington, Delaware, to be with his mother. Cedella Marley says that her son asked her to trim his locks before showing up for the night shift at the plant of the smallest of the Big Three US car manufacturers. Booker complied and tells how she gathered the shorn locks and put them in a paper bag for burial, in keeping, she claims, with the belief of some Rastas that disposing of one's hair clippings in any other way can lead to madness. In reality, most Rastas would rather die then trim, and regard scissors as sacrilegious— "Locks cyaan cut, nevah," says one respected elder, not even, he insists for a needed job at Chrysler.

NIGHT SHIFT

Detroit's Bob Seger wrote a hit song with the same title (as did The Commodores after Marley died) and, as a boy from the Motor City, would probably agree with Marley that the never-ending night shift on a car assembly line is the one thing likely to stay in the mind long after the last time card has been punched.

Wilmington, Delaware was a hostile, if temporary, home for Bob Marley who, like the hundreds of thousands of his countrymen who have journeyed to the cold white north to "make a money", had trouble dealing with winter's frigid temperatures. Marley also didn't like the "rush, rush" of North American life, his mother says, and from her, and other accounts, it was only his music that kept her son moving forward and focused on a future free of Babylon's restraints. "He sat for hours and hours strumming on his acoustic guitar, always coming up with new songs," says Mother Booker, and tells how at one point, because he thought it was bothering his stepfather, he would leave a room whenever the latter entered. Edward Booker, however, was apparently not bothered at all. In fact, confirms Cedella, he found the repetitive guitar chords of his stepson's songwriting relaxing.

'Night Shift', originally recorded for Lee Perry as 'It's All Right', was written during one of those Wilmington songwriting sessions. Opening with the Biblical quote, "The sun shall not smite thee by day, nor the moon by night" (Psalms 121.6), the lyrics cleverly capture the out-of-step confusion of the night worker, and the monotony of manual labour. Still, he concludes, "It's all right, it's gonna be all right"… if not for a while. Laid off from Chrysler, and forced onto the welfare rolls, Marley got his Vietnam draft papers and promptly left the USA to go back to his island home. He would later deny, however, any relation between the two events.

Like 'Cry To Me', 'Night Shift', having been previously recorded, had to be registered as written by Bob Marley, and published by Cayman Music. By contrast, the eight new songs were registered to Bob Marley Music.

MARLEY PERFORMED AT REGGAE SUNSPLASH IN 1979, IN MONTEGO BAY'S JARRETT PARK

WHO THE CAP FIT

Certain of Bob Marley's lyrics have become ingrained into everyday Jamaican speech, and though many of them may not have originated with him, they are now so associated with his name that everyone thinks he created them. So it is with the warning that your worst enemy might be your best friend and your best friend might be your enemy from 'Who The Cap Fit'. Jamaica, as any Jamaican will confirm, is a land of many hypocrites, and a land where the truth is as elusive as pinning down a peeny wally (firefly) on a moonlit May night. No one has ever summed this up better than Bob Marley did in this song.

Robert Nesta Marley did not trust easily. The contrast between country and town is brutal, and the little boy from Brown's Town would have had to learn street smarts in record time just to survive. And learn the rule of the ghetto: "trust no man". Yet, as he himself would later reflect, nothing that he had learned in the tough, zinc-lined lanes of Trench Town would really prepare him for the even tougher world of the Jamaican music business.

A common refrain of Jamaicans is that none keep them down as much as their own. As Bob Marley would discover, the more he succeeded, the more those who controlled the industry would fight him down, a reality made even more insidious by the fact that his enemies never revealed themselves. He, unlike the open-book that was Peter Tosh, also kept the specifics to himself, letting those who had the right head size figure it out for themselves. "People here feel like they must fight against me and I must fight against

GARISH MARLEY
EFFIGY AT THE
BOB MARLEY MUSEUM
IN HOPE ROAD

you… they don't want fe trick you, they want fe trick your mind, that's the thing I don't like," Marley said.

"Bob was the conscience of reggae," believes Tyrone Downie, who goes on to make his own point about who the cap fit today. "If he was alive, there would be no 'Reggae Rum', or other exploitation of him or the music," says the man acknowledged as one of Jamaica's finest keyboard players. Downie also expresses dismay, as do many of the travelers that take in the Bob Marley Museum, that one of the items on sale, and promoted at the entrance gate is "Bobscream", an ice cream in different flavors like 'Rita's Watermelon', 'Stir It Up' and 'Want More'.

The songwriting credit on 'Who The Cap Fit' was given to Family Man Barrett. According to Don Taylor, this was because all of the new songs on *Rastaman Vibration* were registered under names other than Marley's to evade Cayman Music's claim on his publishing, but to Family Man, who explains that the song was "the rewritten 'Man To Man' from Upsetter days", a perfectly legitimate credit. "I officially helped Bob put together ten songs," says the Wailer bassist, and 'Who The Cap Fit' is one of them. "Scratch and Bob put the lyrics together and I changed the arrangement and added the corn phrase ('Said I threw me corn, mi no call me fowl/I saying cok-cok-cok-cluck-cluck-cluck')," which, Family Man explains, "is an ancient rhyme meaning to do the right thing and the guiltiness will rest on the wrongdoer's conscience".

It is an apt lead-in to his next point: "The people who have control are trying to get rid of The Wailers' rights," he complains, and says that he, along with the other remaining Wailers, have been involved in a lawsuit against the Marley Estate for many years for royalties owing to them.

"I was credited for five songs only, and for a long time it was OK with us," he explains, "but it's not OK any more and I'm confident that good will win over evil."

CRY TO ME

Rasta warriors with a militant message aren't supposed to sing about love. When they do, they're accused, somewhat fittingly, of having gone "soft". As the only love song on the *Rastaman Vibration* album, 'Cry To Me' was acceptable only as the exception that proved this Rasta rule.

In the early days of Marley's music (of which 'Cry To Me' was a throwback), the majority of his tunes were love songs, and were accepted as such without judgement. This, however, was before he grew locks and was anointed as prophet, and expected to confine his expression to the serious business at hand.

These attempts to box him into being a conduit for what others wanted, rather than being free to explore his creative complexity, were derisively dismissed by Bob, who would defiantly release the ultra "soft", and commercially very successful, *Kaya* a couple of years later. Like he said, "overcome the devil with a thing called love".

'Cry To Me', a song of betrayal that, a few years down the road, would serve to let wife Rita know how he felt when she bore daughter Stephanie by another man, was originally recorded by The Wailers for Sir Coxsone Dodd, who first released it as a single and then as part of Studio One's critically dismissed collection, *The Best Of Bob Marley And The Wailers*, in 1974.

One of the two songs on *Rastaman Vibration* that, because it was a "do-over", had to be acknowledged registered as a Bob Marley-written song, 'Cry To Me' was published by Cayman Music.

> "Overcome the devil with a thing called love"
> — **Bob Marley**

ROOTS, ROCK, REGGAE

'Roots, Rock, Reggae', a popular term of the time, is nothing more, and nothing less, than a great introductory reggae groove. Marley was fond of quoting his grandmother: "When the root is strong, the fruit is sweet," and said himself that he didn't see "how you can leave your roots". The root of Rasta is Africa; the rock (commonly but erroneously thought to refer to the music) is Jamaica; and reggae represents the combination of the two.

Bob Marley understood the power that comes from synergy and would pull pieces from everywhere to expand on a lyrical concept. Tyrone Downie says that there was always room for addition or change to Wailers' material. Even after a song had been rehearsed for weeks, new lyrics could be added in the studio. "Some songs were ready, but some were finished in the studio. Bob would ask for lyrics—he'd say, 'Tyrone give me a verse', or look to one of the other Wailers for ideas." Chris Blackwell, knowing a good dance tune when he heard it, released this track as an Island Records' single in four different combinations—on the flip side of 'Positive Vibration', 'Cry To Me', 'Who The Cap Fit' and 'Stir It Up'. A co-writing credit on the song was given to Marley's Trench Town link, Vincent 'Tartar' Ford.

SMILE JAMAICA

Not on the *Rastaman Vibration* album, this song was written at Michael Manley's request for an uplifting number to accompany the 1976 musical rally. Marley had agreed to perform on the condition that it wasn't a political event (a naive expectation for a Manley-initiated campaign booster scheduled for two weeks before election day). Answering critics, who questioned his motivation, Marley was curt: "I said 'Smile, you're in Jamaica.' I didn't say 'Smile Jamaicans, be a Jamaican.' I don't deal with that—a whole bag of fuckery that."

'Smile Jamaica' as a positive theme was resurrected, with Jasper Conran-designed T-Shirts, in 1988 when a hurricane relief concert was held in London to aid the victims of "Gilbert". Smiling faces on the island were scarce, however, when four million worth of US dollars, and thousands of yards of zinc, vanished into the Jamaican air without trace before it got anywhere close to the victims it had been intended for.

The title has recently surfaced again as the title of TVJ's (one of Jamaica's two television stations) morning program.

> ## "Smile, you're in Jamaica"
> **– Bob Marley**

OPPOSITE, THE WAILERS IN THE STUDIO

EXODUS

Three Little Birds

Waiting In Vain

Turn Your Lights Down Low

One Love

Natural Mystic

Jamming

Exodus

Guiltiness

The Heathen

So Much Things To Say

DREAD TAKES A DRAW OUTSIDE THE GATES OF MARLEY'S SPECTACULAR BUT NEVER-FINISHED STUDIO AT PORT MARIA

Produced by: Bob Marley And The Wailers

The Natty Dread tour—Bob's solo debut—was a huge success for the man so many were hailing as not only the king of reggae music, but also the hottest new thing in rock (a feat that no other reggae performer has managed to equal).

That Marley had crossed over the line that has always kept reggae acts locked firmly in the ethnic closet, and become so appealing to the fickle rock audience was, in large part, Chris Blackwell's doing. Blackwell believes that a good producer will always have a marketing plan even before going into the studio. "From the outset," he says, "whatever I did was always with a thought to marketing." He continues: "This is why I brought in Wayne (Perkins) and Rabbit for the overdubs on Catch A Fire. I planned to hit with the rock sound, to open up the market. We could then pull back to a more simple (or raw) sound, but first we had to get in the door."

Just before Exodus was released in May of 1977, Bob Marley and Family Man Barrett were charged in a London court with possession of ganja, but were both let off with a light fine (£50 and £20, respectively), and a lecture from a slightly bemused judge. This was one of the very rare instances that herb's biggest promoter was actually held accountable for his open smoking and tireless crusade for the legalisation of weed. "The more people smoke, the more Babylon fall," was his fervent belief.

Exodus, the fifth studio album for Island Records, had as much of a rock influence as the group's first LP for the label and drew additional criticism for being too sophisticated, too international, too far away from Marley's roots (a cardinal sin for reggae musicians). But this particular reggae musician, as always, had a perfect comeback: "Marley's music is always Marley's music. I haven't changed my musical sound. A man plays his music according to the way he feels." What had changed, however, were his musicians. Tyrone Downie—who, due to being raised "with differing music all around me, the church on one side, a sound system on the other" and with Peter Tosh as his neighbour, had a very open mind to new sounds—had taken over some of the arranging from the more conservative Family Man, and in the wake of Al Anderson's departure to play with Peter Tosh's Word, Sound And Power, Junior Marvin was hired.

Marvin, a Jamaican-born British guitarist with a post-Hendrix pop sound brought with him a European sensibility as opposed to the American input of Perkins and Anderson. He remembers being impressed by Marley's professionalism and was immediately made aware by the group's leader that he was expected to follow his strict example.

In retrospect, Exodus sounds as roots reggae as it comes, and is, of all Marley albums, the one where all of his many sides worked together for the first time, but in the disco-happy Seventies, the music on this set was considered very radical, a quality that could have been the reason why the elusive black audience Marley had been courting since the Sixties suddenly started to listen. It was the title track of Exodus, which, with its urgent Afrocentric lyrics, was added to R&B playlists and which, when released as a single, was bought in good numbers by the black community.

The small but growing interest of the hard-to-crack R&B audience was helped greatly by the interest and support of Stevie Wonder (who was so drawn to reggae that, in the early Eighties, he moved into the Intercontinental Hotel in Ocho Rios for several months, taking the hotel's resident reggae band, Happiness Unlimited, back to California with him when he left). Wonder developed a relationship with Marley and performed with him on at least two occasions. His tribute song to his friend, 'Master Blaster Jammin'' is not only an acknowledgement of Marley's power, but a prophetic hint that one day the blacks of both Jamaica and the USA would unite through music (a thought most would have dismissed as ridiculous at the time).

The Bob Marley And The Wailers tour of continental Europe started immediately after Exodus hit the streets, and the tour's success was duplicated in a multi-date engagement at north London's Rainbow Theatre. Momentum was picking up daily—Jamaican artist, Nancy Burke, who was part of Marley's London entourage, describes it as "an energy so intense it seemed it would never end". But suddenly there was a problem that would bring this phenomenon to a close, and much sooner than anyone could have imagined.

In 1975, Marley had injured his toe playing football. Asked about it in 1977 he said, "In Paris, I was playing soccer and a man gave me a rasclaat tackle in the rain. The foot started paining me and I wonder… why it burn for so

> "The more people smoke herb, the more Babylon fall"
>
> **– Bob Marley**

long. I score a goal and just hop off the field. When I took off my shoe, the toenail was completely out."

Ignoring medical advice at the time to refrain from further football, Marley continued indulging in his second most important passion. Staying in London's Oakley Street, a location picked especially because of its close proximity to soccer-friendly Battersea Park, Marley made the game a part of his daily routine. During one of these casual matches, another skirmish with a player resulted in his toe being reinjured by his opponent's rusty cleats. Once again, Marley kept on kicking, giving the toe no chance to heal.

On July 7, 1977, a day foretold in Rasta theology to be the "Two Sevens Clash", or a day of serious import, Denise Mills took Bob to a Harley Street specialist. Mills who, after single-handedly running Island's Jamaican affairs from her vine-covered, white cottage overlooking Ocho Rios Bay for many years, would herself die at a young age from emphysema in 1995. She remained reluctant to talk about Bob's illness, even after several years had elapsed since his death. But she did say that no one—least of all she and Bob—had any inkling on that hot July day that the toe would not be easily treated.

Looking back, perhaps it could have been. The British doctor recommended amputation, but Marley, thinking he would have difficulty performing without the toe, opted instead to cancel the US leg of his tour, fly to Miami and live in a newly-purchased villa with his mother for five months. He also consulted another doctor while in Florida who told him that a skin graft would save the toe.

In a fateful decision, Marley opted for the less drastic solution, a choice that would ultimately cost him his life.

THREE LITTLE BIRDS

On one of Kingston's main thoroughfares sits 56 Hope Road, in a good residential area of town that is full of fruit trees, flowers and birds. Written on the back step of Hope Road, where Marley sat for many an hour picking out tunes on his guitar, and trying out lyrics ("It used to sound like gibberish at first," says Cindy Breakespeare, "but he'd sing it over and over and words would begin to come… then someone would hit a matchbox or teacup and the song would start to gel"). 'Three Little Birds' is believed to have been inspired by three small ground doves that would hang out by Bob's doorstep. The birds were attracted by the steady supply of seeds discarded during the ritual of herb cleaning,

MARLEY INDULGING IN ONE OF HIS THREE PASSIONS—THE OTHER TWO BEING MUSIC AND WOMEN

which, for the Rastaman, is almost as important as the rolling of the spliff and the sacramental smoking of the holy herb.

Almost certainly the inspiration for Bobby McFerrin's Eighties hit, 'Don't Worry', 'Three Little Birds', with its simple advice and reassurance ("Don't worry about a thing, 'cos every little thing's gonna be OK") has helped many a despondent ghetto dweller through another hard Jamaican day, and become a staple of the now almost extinct three-man calypso groups which, with their homemade rhythm boxes, maracas, and acoustic guitars were once such an integral part of the tourist experience.

"It used to sound like gibberish at first, but he'd sing it over and over and words would begin to come"

– Cindy Breakespeare

WAITING IN VAIN

Arguably Marley's best and most played love song (vying only with 'Could You Be Loved?' for top spot), 'Waiting In Vain' begs the question, "Who was it written for?" (Don Taylor says that Cindy Breakespeare—before she became Bob's girl—was the elusive woman he didn't want to waste time on, but it's not one of the songs she takes inspirational credit for), and the soulful vocal of a man so intrigued by the chase that the capture has to be a letdown, never fails to affect the listener because of its wistful honesty.

"Women were always throwing themselves at his feet," says Cindy Breakespeare, who despite her long and close relationship with the singer was described by him as "one of my girlfriends". Breakespeare, early on, adopted the policy of "giving him his space", and it was a space that was rarely vacant. From pauper to princess (of Gabon), Marley had them all. Yet it was only Rita Marley who captured, and kept, the post of his legal "queen".

Like most Rastamen, Marley was attracted to the women of "Babylon", those who wore makeup and dressed in jeans and minidresses. But he was also true to his Rasta faith in that he would admonish his women that a bare face was beautiful, and a frock far more in keeping with women's rightful role. Keeping women barefoot, pregnant and in the kitchen (except when menstruating, at which time women are required to keep their distance from all food preparation) is a practiced principle of Rasta doctrine. "I had to ask if I was ready to throw away my razor and nail polish," says Breakespeare, who also remembers trying unsuccessfully to hide the fact that she wore makeup from her musician boyfriend.

Who Marley was yearning for in this song will never be known, but as his wife, Rita, ruefully recalls that, "Bob loved to be seen as a lover, not just as a rebel."

TURN YOUR LIGHTS DOWN LOW

On a sunny January morning, Cindy Breakespeare sits sipping strong coffee in the eclectic and charming Stony Hill apartment that she and new husband, musician and air pilot, Rupert Bent Sr, share. "'Turn Your Lights Down Low' was written for me at Hope Road," she confides. Breakespeare, looking, in her long cotton print dress with face free of make-up, very much in synch with Rasta dress codes, admits that it was initially hard for her to consider dating a dread. Having attended Immaculate Conception High School—still considered the best of the Kingston's many all-girl secondary schools, and so proper that its students wear petticoats under their white uniforms—she was taught, in the Rasta-phobic Seventies, that if an

Immaculate girl saw a Rastaman coming towards them they were to cross the road and "keep our eyes straight ahead". "Rastaman were said to be mad," she says. It's not surprising that Cindy Breakespeare found the forbidden enticing. "It was a very exciting time in Jamaica for those who understood the Rasta culture." For those who didn't, it was very threatening.

In its beginning, the Rasta philosophy was very seductive and, as its foremost practitioner, Bob Marley was a master seducer. Whatever the topic, Marley's music seduced. It pulled you in and held you spellbound by its positive alternative to a largely negative world. 'Turn Your Lights Down Low' is a lighter example of Marley's musical might, but shows how powerful a simple love song can be.

RITA MARLEY IN
1982, ONE YEAR
AFTER HER
HUSBAND'S DEATH

ONE LOVE

> ## "Me don' dip on the black man's side nor the white man's side, me dip on God's side"
>
> **– Bob Marley**

The Rasta of the Nineties is more intent on burning down than building bridges, and the original "one love" dread is fast becoming an endangered species as the militant Bobo dreads take control of the faith. The Bobos, a sub-sect of Rastafari whose members believe in confining their locks under tight turbans as much as the Rastas of the Seventies and Eighties believed in flashing them, and who preach insurrection as much as Marley preached love, were once confined to a very small community in Bull Bay (a few miles outside Kingston where Bob Marley once housed his wife and children). Traditionally supporting themselves by selling handmade brooms at busy Kingston intersections, as well as door-to-door, the Bobos have diversified of late into the more lucrative entertainment business, and have led the Rasta movement for the past five years, creating a rift between them and other branches of the faith.

"Unity is the world's key to racial harmony," said Marley. "Until the white man stops calling himself white, and the black man stops calling himself black, we will not see it. All the people on earth are just one family." He also made clear that "Me don' dip on the black man's side, nor the white man's side, me dip on God's side."

In the years since the reggae bard's death, 'One Love' has been used by the Jamaica Tourist Board to sell Jamaica in prime-time ads on CNN. The high-budget commercial presents Jamaica as a land of love, peace and harmony. "Out of many one people" is indeed the island's motto, but it is an ideal still waiting to be realized.

Marley recorded several other versions of 'One Love', including a 12-inch remix fusing into the original recording parts of Curtis Mayfield's 'People Get Ready' to emphasize the song's plea.

PRODUCER CLEMENT 'SIR COXSONE' DODD, WHOSE STUDIO ONE LABEL WAS RESPONSIBLE FOR 'SIMMER DOWN', THE WAILERS' FIRST HIT IN 1964

Being a "relic" of the original Coxsone Dodd track, this is the work that most embodies the message of Bob Marley: "One love, one heart, let's get together and feel all right". And although Jamaica's official national anthem is 'Jamaica Land We Love', it is 'One Love' that the world sings when it wants to make a point. The title has also made its way into the Jamaican language as a righteous way to greet or leave someone.

But sadly the "one love" sentiment that proved so magnetic to Marley's followers passed on with its creator.

NATURAL MYSTIC

Perry Henzell, director of the cult classic, *The Harder They Come*, once said of Jamaica that its mysterious energy is the result of the island being a "red hot" connector between the cultures of Africa and North America, and anyone who has felt this energy's presence can vouch for its existence. Surrender to it and it will take you on a journey you'll never forget. Marley called this phenomenon the "natural mystic", but the song may also have had a more personal interpretation. "I believe he was the 'natural mystic'. I think he was singing about himself," posits Cindy Breakespeare, who names this track as her favourite—"Whenever I hear it, it makes me feel a way."

Jamaica's spiritual centre is a complex mix of Pocomania, Pentecostal, Catholicism, Anglican and Rastafari, and when these elements converge strange things happen, none of which can be explained. "Those who feel it, know it," is Rita Marley's explanation. Dave Tollington, senior vice president of Warner Music, and former disc jock at Toronto's groundbreaking radio station, CHUM-FM, who remembers clearly being rooted

to the spot the first time he heard Bob Marley in the mid-Seventies, and who has made countless pilgrimages to Jamaica since then, and Sting, who wrote many of the songs on his *The Dream Of The Blue Turtles* album in Jamaica, also claims to have felt the vibe.

EDWARD SEAGA, PRIME MINISTER OF JAMAICA FROM 1980 TO 1988 AND EARLY RECORD PRODUCER

JAMMING

As recently as the April 1999 gas riots, it was written in the local press, and repeated on many radio stations, that it is the poor that bear the burden of keeping Jamaica afloat. Other classes may have suffered increased hardship as the country's economy drifts closer and closer on its sea of corruption to complete bankruptcy, but it is the "massive" who suffer the most.

"We are the living sacrifice," sang the man who, although he moved to a much better address, never really left the ghetto, "and we're jammin' right straight from yard", in a song that unites the two main components of his music—joy and Jah. Released in a 12-inch version that was a 1977 club hit, 'Jamming' is one of

those rare songs with a religious theme that is also hailed as great to dance to. 'Jamming' was also the song that the Gong was singing when he called the warring politicians Michael Manley and Edward Seaga onstage during the memorable One Love concert, and got them to shake hands—a moment re-played in the minds of many Jamaicans when Seaga (who is still opposition leader as he was in 1978, after being prime minister from 1980–1988), and Manley's one-time mentor, Fidel Castro, attended the former leader's Kingston funeral in 1997. Seaga, who also attended (and spoke at) Marley's funeral, paid silent tribute to his old enemy as he stood quietly, head bowed, beside his coffin with none of their one-time bitter rivalry evident.

EXODUS

The album's title had been chosen by The Skipper before this title track was written. Exiled as he was in Nassau, Marley equated his forced exit from Jamaica with the departure of the Israelites from Egypt. It was the movement of Jah people—out of Babylon and forward to The Promised Land.

Repatriation to his spiritual home remained a big part of Marley's vision until he passed on. "Today is not the day," he said in 1976, "but when it happen, 144,000 of us go home." Twelve tribes of 12,000—Reuben, Simeon, Levi, Judah, Issachar, Zebulun, Dan, Gad, Asher, Naphtali, Joseph and Benjamin—all going home to Zion. (The reggae star himself was, because of his February birth, a member of the tribe of Joseph, and was believed by some people, including Judy Mowatt, to be a reincarnation of Joseph himself).

'Exodus' was hailed by Marley's label as the first single to be picked up by black radio stations in North America, and the Caribbean's star's US audiences began to reflect this breakthrough. By the late Seventies, his audiences had broadened beyond the hip (and in many cases well-off) whites who had been with him from the beginning, to the urban black community he had long wooed without being noticed.

Like other great songwriters, Marley saw himself only as a conduit, a channeler of Jah's word to the masses – "It is not me saying these things, it's God… if God hadn't given me a song to sing, I wouldn't have a song to sing."

> "It is not me saying these things, it's God… if God hadn't given me a song to sing, I wouldn't have a song to sing"
> **– Bob Marley**

GUILTINESS

When in the studio, Bob Marley spoke little (and laughed even less), but communicated constantly with the other musicians through facial expressions and body movements.

By the time *Exodus* was recorded, Marley and his Wailers had developed a tight musical rapport, and before any Wailers' song was recorded it had been rehearsed so often that few takes were required. Everyone associated with Bob Marley—engineers, musicians, family, friends, manager, label executives—all mention his discipline and his devotion to rehearsal.

"He was a perfectionist," Breakespeare notes, a view echoed by Chris Blackwell, Don Taylor and many others. Marley's take on his work habits was simple: "I have a job to do and want to do it well."

'Guiltiness' is not one of the reggae icon's better-known compositions. Its admonition to the "downpressors" (Rasta-speak for "oppressors"), the "big fish who always try to eat… the small fish" is a truism that is, in the Jamaican experience, timeless. The slave masters have merely been replaced by an even more insidious system that imprisons the poor as effectively as the strongest iron chains.

The *Exodus* album contains many references to guilt and innocence and the confusion between the two. It is a truism that the island's justice system, despite being based on British law, is heavily biased against the poor, and that "guilty until proven innocent" is the maxim that guides most arrests (or killings) of not only ghetto residents, but anyone who doesn't have friends in high places.

> ## "I have a job to do and want to do it well"
> – Bob Marley

THE HEATHEN

Even before the advent of Rastafari, Jamaica was one of the most devout nations on the planet, its high number of churches competing only, ironically, with its equally impressive number of bars. Yet, still the heathen flourishes. Like nowhere else on earth, good and evil are in constant battle for control of this beautiful isle. And it is this duality in the national character that gives Jamaica its sometimes dangerous, and deadly fascinating edge, setting up a creative tension that so often is stretched beyond normal breaking point, but somehow never actually snaps.

To be called "heathen" in Jamaica is as bad as, or worse than, being called a "batty man" (gay). Society's rules are simple and are based on a literal interpretation of the Bible's Old Testament. People are regularly stoned, chopped or beaten to death for crimes that in other societies are dealt with legally and far less severely, like theft. Heathens, whether real or imagined, are not so drastically disposed of, but they are shunned by all.

Perhaps fittingly, given a tendency in Jamaica to view rock music suspiciously, 'The Heathen' is the song on *Exodus* that has the most rock guitar on it. Junior Marvin gives the track an almost ominous feel, which reinforces Marley's lyrics quite effectively.

SO MUCH THINGS TO SAY

Invoking the names of Jesus and Jamaican national heroes, Marcus Garvey and slave leader Paul Bogle, as examples of how wrong "they" can be in their pursuit of "right", Marley wrote this song around the time that he was arrested for possession of pot, and while he was being regularly harassed by the police, often just for being Bob Marley.

Ever conscious of the Jamaican love for fighting each other down and the tendency to rejoice more in a man's failure than in his success, Marley uses the Rasta term I'n'I ("I" and the Creator are one) to both stand apart from the naysayers and to expose them.

The irie groove of 'So Much Things To Say' moves feet instantly, while the lyrics move minds over time, a characteristic of Marley's best work. "When he was in the studio, he was so disciplined," says Junior Tucker, who spent several of his formative years hanging out with the Marleys at Hope Road. "There were such high standards in those days… everyone was under pressure to live up to US

standards, and because there was never a big enough budget to do this, there was no wasting of studio time. Bob led the pack when it came to rehearsal, and being ready to record when you walked in the studio." Tucker's observations about Marley's commitment to rehearsal are echoed by many and by the time a song like 'So Much Things To Say' got to studio stage, each musician would know his parts thoroughly. Very few of The Wailers' songs ever evolved from a studio jam.

Yet even with Bob Marley's zest for technical perfection, an acceptable final take still came down to the vibe. And sometimes, the music laid down just wouldn't suit The Skipper."

His was a very simple approach to music," notes Tucker, reminiscing about the days he sat in on The Wailers' sessions. "He would say 'the music vex' or 'the music happy'. If it 'vex', the band would have to work until they heard him say 'the music right now', looking at his musicians as they answered 'yes Skip', 'yes Skip'."

NATIONAL HERO AND BLACK RIGHTS ADVOCATE MARCUS MOSIAH GARVEY

KAYA

Time Will Tell

Is This Love?

Kaya

Satisfy My Soul

Sun Is Shining

Easy Skanking

Misty Morning

She's Gone

Running Away

Crisis

1978

Produced by: Bob Marley
And The Wailers

"Really I am just a man of the people" – Bob Marley

In early 1978, the People's National Party—and its constituency—was in serious trouble. The politically-engineered social unrest that had been seething throughout the small island for the past several years was in grave danger of erupting, and everyone was predicting a painful outcome.

Bob Marley, still in the self-chosen exile brought about by the 1976 Hope Road shooting, was in London when he was contacted by three of his political cohorts —Claude Massop, Bucky Marshall and Tony Welch—and asked if he would appear at a planned Kingston peace concert dubbed "One Love" (both a Rasta greeting and an expression of unity). Marley, who had been working on what would be his *Kaya* album, agreed to return for the show.

The One Love Peace Concert held under a full tropical moon on April 22, 1978, at Kingston's National Stadium, was the musical event of the Jamaican year. With Bob Marley and his Wailers, and a 16-act supporting roster that included Peter Tosh (who, during his performance, in typical Tosh fashion, lit up a huge ganja spliff in blatant and unchallenged disregard of the heavy police presence), the venue, which was surrounded by armed security forces, was packed with people from all levels of Jamaican society, and from all corners of the troubled island, including Prime Minister Michael Manley and opposition leader Edward Seaga. Everyone, including Mick Jagger, who was in Kingston visiting Peter Tosh, wanted to see Bob Marley, and everyone was ready for peace.

One of the artists appearing that night was 12-year-old Junior Tucker. Tucker remembers the night for what he believes was "the best performance of Bob's life", and tells how when The Skipper walked to the stage from his bus "he was the most high I had ever seen him… he was charged". While Marley was performing, Tucker sat on the side of the stage mesmerized. "It was awesome," he recalls. Chris Blackwell, according to the young singer, disagreed with Tucker's assessment, and didn't rate his protégé's performance that night too highly. "It was the first time Bob used horns in Jamaica and Chris didn't like them," Tucker says, a memory Blackwell confirms.

The undisputed highlight of the One Love Peace Concert, and a scene that has become almost a cliché in Jamaican music history, was the moment when Marley, in the middle of 'Jamming', called on both Manley and Seaga to join him on stage. Skanking dervish-like, his movements in synch with Carly Barrett's inimitable one-drop drumbeat—and the significance of the moment dramatically accentuated by simulated thunder and lightning—Marley ad-libbed a mixture of both song and speech until the two casually dressed leaders, both looking a little sheepish, stood, one on each side of him, and allowed the reggae icon to join their hands above his head to his loud and triumphant utterance of "One love", followed by the equally exuberant call and response of "Jah Rastafari".

Before Marley had traveled back to Jamaica at the end of February, he and The Wailers had recorded most of the tracks for the *Kaya* album (named after the once-popular street slang for ganja) at the Fallout Shelter at Island's headquarters in St Peter's Square. A much softer, and more commercial, set of tunes than Wailers fans were accustomed to, the expectation was that Bob would be accused of selling out—and he was. Adamant that he be allowed the freedom to explore different styles, Marley told an interviewer that "when we was doing *Kaya* we knew that plenty people was gonna say *Kaya*, blah, blah, blah, but we still do it, you know." He also held fast to his belief that an artist must lead, rather than follow the crowd. "If you start follow the crowd, bwoy, bad t'ing." He also made the cogent observation that (given the sensitive timing) a "soft" selection of songs wasn't such a bad idea. "Maybe if I'd tried to make (an album) heavier than *Kaya*, they would have assassinated me… these things are heavier than anyone can understand."

Cindy Breakespeare, the Canadian-born former Miss World (1978) who became the reggae star's lover and "baby modda", bearing his youngest son—Damian—(and who still lives in Kingston with her husband, jazz guitarist/airline pilot Rupert Bent, in a stylishly eclectic third-floor apartment atop posh Stony Hill), believes that some of the songs on *Kaya* were written about her. And, since several Marley intimates including manager, Don Taylor, confirm that he was smitten with her at the time, she's probably right. But *Kaya* is also a tribute to another love of the Rastaman's life—the ever-present spliff of sensemillia.

Pretty women and potent herb were as important

to Robert Nesta Marley as politics and his quest for local—and world—peace. In this context, *Kaya* is as valid an album as *Survival*, but Marley was more than ready for the mixed response: "Too much romance with Miss Breakespeare," he laughed to Cindy, "ca' me is a militant yout'." But, regardless of the controversy, *Kaya* went to Number 4 in the UK charts during the week of its release. And Chris Blackwell says that *Kaya* is his favorite album, because, he says, "it's full of joy".

This complimentary assessment of the controversial album contrasts sharply with Don Taylor's assertion that Blackwell didn't intend to put the album out because it was too "soft" (a catch-all Jamaican phrase for anything that isn't happening).

In addition to its local significance, the One Love concert was thought of as an appropriate, if unofficial, opening date for The Wailers' first world tour, which, after their usual successful swing through Europe, produced another live album, this one a double set called *Babylon By Bus*, taking its title from a review written in London's influential music rag, the *New Musical Express*. Capturing the extraordinary energy that had left European fans on a great high, *Babylon By Bus* contained tracks like 'Lively Up Yourself' (which also appeared on *Live!*), 'Is This Love', 'No More Trouble', 'Positive Vibration' and 'Punky Reggae Party'.

'Punky Reggae Party' had been recorded in London's Hammersmith studio in the early summer of 1977 for Lee "Scratch" Perry. This was the year that punk rock was emerging as England's dominant music force, and though at first somewhat skeptical about its message, Marley, appreciative of punk's use of reggae rhythm, soon embraced the music's rebellious stance. Taking his cue from groups like The Clash (last seen in Jamaica in 1982 wearing very un-punklike woven palm leaf hats, decorated with bobbing birds) he began to incorporate a little of punk's outrageous attitude into his own work. "In a way," he said, "Me like to see dem safety pins an' t'ing. Me nah do it miself, but mi like see a man can suffer without crying."

At the session was the three-man British reggae group, Aswad (Brinsley Forde, Tony Gad, and Drummer Zeb), Cat Coore on guitar and Ibo Cooper on organ. Perry that day was "jumping around the studio, doing little dances and all of a sudden creating parts which separately made no sense, but which came together in a kind of counter-melody marriage. Perry weaves a very

THE ONE LOVE PEACE CONCERT IN KINGSTON WHERE MARLEY JOINED THE WARRING HANDS OF MANLEY AND EDWARD SEAGA

good tapestry." As for Bob Marley, Cooper, himself an inspiration to many, describes him as "very inspiring… he went nine hours with neither spliff nor food. He just stayed in the (vocal) booth and kept on singing." At the end of these nine long hours, Perry went home with two outstanding tracks: 'Punky Reggae Party' and 'Keep On Moving'. Both of these songs were to become staples of the singer's live shows.

With Europe done and *Babylon By Bus* out and selling, the next focus was the United States, and after some initial problems getting Junior Marvin into the country because of an old drugs charge, the tour got off to a slightly-delayed but welcomed start in North America on May 19, 1978 in Cleveland, Ohio.

The tour arrived in Toronto, Canada, on a balmy Friday night on June 9, Marley playing the famous, and recently closed, 20,000-seater Maple Leaf Gardens, and the audience, a mixed bag of black and white united under a sea of red, green and gold tams, T-shirts, scarves, buttons and beads, was as responsive to Marley's hypnotic music as if born to the one-drop beat. When Bob said, "Jah!", the crowd roared "Rastafari", and when the

concert ended and hundreds of people boarded the northbound subway car at Yonge and College, an impromptu passenger version of 'One Love' carried the train not to its intended destination of Finch Avenue, but, instead, straight to Zion.

When the tour reached Madison Square Gardens, the *New York Times* critic hailed the sold-out concert as "a triumph… for reggae in general, and for Mr Marley in particular". A few months later, Marley was honoured in New York by the United Nations which presented him with a Medal of Peace.

Following the last date in America, Marley briefly returned to Jamaica, linking up with his longtime producer and friend, Scratch Perry for a short studio session during which he recorded four songs. Island's reggae star was able to do this because, as the first Jamaican artist to enjoy a properly negotiated contract, he had retained "Caribbean rights", or

THE CLASH, A PUNK GROUP WHOSE MUSIC OWED MUCH TO THE INFLUENCE OF REGGAE

"Maybe if I'd tried to make an album heavier than Kaya, they'd have assassinated me"

– Bob Marley

SOCCER PLAYER
ALAN 'SKILL' COLE,
MARLEY'S FRIEND
AND CONFIDANTE

the right to record himself, or for other producers, and to distribute any such Wailers material throughout that territory on his own label. It was a way of not only controlling the group's output in their own region, but also of maintaining a critical presence in their home market.

Marley was glad of his short respite "back a yard". Ahead was The Wailers' first tour of Australia, New Zealand and the Far East. No one was sure how this group of serious-looking musical messengers from Jamaica, the first reggae act ever to perform on such alien shores would be received. As it turned out, no one need have worried. When The Wailers' plane, running one-and-a-half hours late, touched down in Sydney at about 11:00pm on a damp and drizzly night, the Aussies were eager to welcome the band to a new and appreciative audience down under. And in both Australia and New Zealand—but especially the latter—the group's usual white fans were joined by the continent's indigenous inhabitants who, in Auckland, met Marley's plane and bestowed upon him a native name meaning "redeemer". These native people gravitated naturally to The Wailers music (as indeed the Hopi Indians would in the United States) as though it was meant for them.

Japan was equally receptive to reggae's alluring beat and its seductive leader (although not at all receptive to the weed that went with it, a restriction that Don Taylor had to get around by carrying his client's supply into the country in his shoes). It was an interest in Jamaica and its music that was to grow steadily from this first introduction in 1978 and last until the

mid-Nineties when it died off during the dancehall-induced stagnation of Jamaica's once unstoppable music production.

But back in the late Seventies, no music was newer and more exciting than reggae and the excitement generated at The Wailers' Tokyo show lit a spark that led thousands of young Japanese fans on a pilgrimage to the Caribbean island home of Robert Nesta Marley, some of whom would stay on, living and working with the people and learning patois—all the better they would shyly admit "to understand what Bob Marley say".

After a couple of other stops—including Hawaii—the 1978 tour ended in Nassau. With the end in sight, the tired Wailers could take great satisfaction in having taken their music right around a globe that was still skanking in the tour's wake.

The final significant event of this busy year was that Robert Marley—following his friend Skill Cole, who had left Jamaica for Ethiopia in 1996—made what for him was a holy pilgrimage, his very first visit to the African continent.

Although he, and manager Don Taylor who had accompanied him, reportedly stayed in Ethiopia with Skill Cole for only four days (the same length of time that Haile Selassie spent in Jamaica), the visit actually reinforced Marley's Rastafarian belief in repatriation, and inspired some of his best work, including 'Zimbabwe', as well as, says Taylor, a plan to one day build a $4 million settlement for the Rastas resident in Ethiopia.

TIME WILL TELL

Family Man Barrett says 'Time Will Tell' was written by "me an' Bob in Nassau", where the band had gone to escape further attacks on Marley's life. The most serious song in the *Kaya* collection came about during a makeshift session in Chris Blackwell's house. "We set up the drums and a tape machine… I was the engineer," says Barrett, "and between us the lyrics and music came together."

The "strange acoustic piano" at the beginning of the song sets its mood, and is, says drummer Barrett, him playing keyboards while "imagining how Fats Domino would do it." Barrett also says that many of the quirky little keyboard bits heard on other songs were his, too. "Sometimes, as arranger, I used to add to Tyrone's keys."

'Time Will Tell' boasts one of the best remembered of Bob Marley's lines, "Think you're in heaven but you're really in hell", a perfect allegory for the two sides of Jamaica. From the pretend paradise of the island's idyllic northcoast to the grim nightmare of the ghetto, heaven and hell, had, by the late Seventies, become interchangeable. As for the main message of the song, it was a warning meant not for the gunmen "who run come crucify the dread", but for the powerful "baldheads" who "set them up".

Released as it was in 1978, time was already telling. The border of the political war zones of Kingston's inner city were becoming blurred in a cloud of shared ganja smoke. Beginning to see the senselessness of politically-encouraged slaughter, the opposing factions of the ghetto had begun to reason. A peace council had been established, and it was as part of this movement that the One Love Peace Concert had been organized. But, as soon as an informal truce had been called, it began to fall apart. Peace was the last thing the politicians actually wanted.

> "Think you're in heaven but you're really in hell"
> **– Bob Marley**

IS THIS LOVE?

One of the two songs on *Kaya* which charted— 'Satisfy My Soul' being the other one—'Is This Love?' is one of those enduring love songs that is covered endlessly in Jamaica by northcoast hotel bands whose target audience is the steady flow of casual, mixed-color couples who meet and make out—probably on a single hotel bed. And it was one of the main songs in the repertoire of a magical band called Happiness Unlimited (resident band at the Intercontinental Hotel in Ocho Rios in 1981), that convinced Stevie Wonder first to jam with them, then to sign them, and finally to take them back to LA.

If the central inspiration was Cindy Breakespeare, then the story begins with their meeting. "We met at 56 Hope Road," she says. "I was renting an apartment downstairs (from Chris Blackwell) and lived there with my brother. Bob (by then her new landlord) and me kept passing each other in the garden. One day he stopped to talk, and that was it." Still a teenager, Breakespeare says that she was "at an age when attachments come easily". Yet she knew instinctively that this flirtation was different: "I said to myself, "Get involved with this dude and he'll change your life for ever." Don Taylor says he knew something was afoot when "Cindy stopped paying rent", and maintains that Breakespeare was not only the true love of Bob Marley's life, but the only woman he respected.

In Jamaica, beauty queens (especially Miss Worlds) are afforded a much higher social status than musicians (no matter how famous), and Breakespeare, used as she was to the social mores of uptown, admits that Marley's expectations required some consideration. "I had to ask myself if I was ready to throw away my razor and nail polish—Bob lived his Rasta philosophy and liked his women natural."

KAYA

'Kaya' was one of the songs originally recorded for Scratch Perry who later did a dub version of the tune for his *Soul Revolution II* (an album released in Jamaica as a limited edition and now very rare). Seventeen-year-old Steven Stanley was the engineer for the dub session which was held in late February, 1978, at the Chin Loy-owned Aquarius Studio in Kingston's Half Way Tree. "Bob," he says, "let Scratch control everything… he was mostly in the back smoking, he didn't say much at all." Marley, who, after the 1976 attempt to take his life no longer liked to travel alone in Jamaica, arrived at Aquarius (dressed as usual "in a jeans suit") with his political posse—in this instance, Claudie Massop, Bucky Marshall and a few other people who were, in Stanley's words, "nevah too right". It wasn't long before word got around that Bob Marley was back in a Jamaican studio and the small Aquarius space was suddenly "corked" with curious onlookers. Bob Marley, says Stanley, had time for all of them—"He just kept smoking."

The Aquarius session lasted all day and not once did Marley inject himself into the mix. Scratch didn't know the board (Aquarius was the first studio in Jamaica to offer a 24-track board—a Rosser custom built) so he had Stanley balance and then "punched in and out to get whatever dub effect he wanted", relates the renowned Stanley, who then tells an interesting post-session story of being driven home by Claudie Massop in the JLP don's black BMW and getting stopped en route by police who started to search the car. "When someone on the street 'tell the police is who,'" Stanley laughs, "dem stop search and tell Claudie dem jus' a pull 'im leg."

No longer a popular term for weed, the word "kaya" has been re-defined as a Marley album title. This song is saying that it was herb that got The Skipper (whose favourite type of herb was lamsbread or Jerusalembread aka goatshit) through a lot of rainy days—the term outlasts definitions.

LEE 'SCRATCH' PERRY, A LEGEND IN HIS OWN TIME (AND MIND!)

SATISFY MY SOUL

Bob Marley liked to do new versions of his old songs and many of the tracks featured on The Wailers' ten Island albums were first recorded as singles for early producers like Scratch Perry. 'Satisfy My Soul' was originally done for Perry (when it was known as 'Don't Rock The Boat' as well as 'I Like It Like This').

With this new version, Marley took back the publishing rights. But it is now believed that Perry did contribute to the writing of some of the Wailer songs he produced.

SUN IS SHINING

'Sun Is Shining', another *Kaya* track first produced by Lee Scratch Perry and released as 'To The Rescue', was written in Wilmington, Delaware, when Marley was living with his mother and doing one of several menial jobs he held under the pseudonym, Donald Marley.

From *Kaya*'s reference to "rain is falling", this song offers a more optimistic take on life, and where ganja got him through the rain, memories of the morning sun—a powerful and positive reminder of Jamaica's blessings—kept him going through a numbing week of work in a cold country far from home.

Arguably the best-mixed track on the album, Chris Blackwell and Robert Ash have created a haunting, dub-enhanced version of a song that is best listened to while driving in a convertible with the top down along Jamaica's comely coastline, on one of those lazy, lovely days that can make Jamaica seem like Eden.

The recording of 'Sun Is Shining' followed much the same pattern as most of Island's Bob Marley And The Wailers catalogue. In the early days when they were still recording in Jamaica, The Wailers would start with an acoustic guitar, a rhythm box and a scratch vocal, before laying down four "bed" tracks—drums, bass, piano and rhythm guitar. By the time they had switched their main recording venue to the UK, the basic rhythm tracks had expanded from four to ten or 11. They added more drums, percussion and lead guitar, and from *Kaya* on, horns as well.

> "Bob was mostly in the back smoking. He didn't say much at all... he just kept smoking"
> — **Steven Stanley, engineer**

EASY SKANKING

For the uninitiated, skanking is a slow dance best done when stoned. And for a time, in the late Seventies, it seemed like the whole island was skanking in steady and sensual unison. The spoilers of this enchanted and, surprisingly—despite the endemic violence—still innocent world, were the police, who had orders to stop-search, prosecute and then ask questions later.

As the decade neared its end, the Rastafarian movement, with its primary focus on peace, was, for a country controlled by tribal warfare, getting alarmingly strong, and efforts by authorities to undermine the Rasta culture intensified.

Roadblocks, manned by both police and M-16-toting soldiers, were everywhere, and "possession" was interpreted on the scene.

Many reggae artists including Bob Marley ignored the danger of open smoking (Peter Tosh going to jail for his defiance). But, unlike Tosh who tended to taunt, Marley was subtle. "Excuse me while I light my spliff," was his gentle way of telling Babylon to go to hell.

> "Excuse me, while I light my spliff," was Bob's gentle way of telling Babylon to go to hell

MISTY MORNING

The island of Jamaica is most beautiful—and most addictive—on misty Blue Mountain mornings when you "don't see no sun", but the mist is a comforting buffer between you and the real world that is slowly waking up around you.

'Misty Morning' was written by a homesick Marley while he was in Delaware toiling for the money which he eventually used to start his own small label. He was later to say that he missed waking up in Jamaica—missed the feeling of knowing you're "back a yard" as the night croak of the tree frogs gives way to the ubiquitous cock crowing that heralds the start of every Jamaican day.

He also missed Cindy Breakespeare, who ended up living with him at various times while he was recording in London. Of time spent with him in the studio, she says that she was "like a fly on the wall". When Marley was working he only had time for his music.

SHE'S GONE

Not many women left Bob Marley. He, not she, was the one who was usually gone. There was always another pretty woman waiting patiently in the wings. For a man who considered marriage a trap, it is likely that lines like "she felt like a prisoner that needs to be free" told more about him than any of his "plenty women". And although he and wife Rita were leading separate lives for many years before his death, Rita Marley's amazing tolerance makes Hilary Clinton's staying power look tame. Asked just after what would have been her husband's 54th birthday how her husband's lasting infidelity had affected her, Rita's reply to the Jamaican entertainment reporter was stoical but honest: "I am a normal woman and things can happen that depress you."

The musical arrangement of 'She's Gone' harkens back to the Sixties sound of Jamaica. The echo chamber effect on the vocal is a throwback to early toasters like URoy and Errol Scorcher, and gives the words a plaintive resonance that communicates pain.

Whether his or hers is a question that will never be answered.

> "She felt like a prisoner that needs to be free"
> **– Bob Marley**

BOB MARLEY WITH
TWO OF THE I'THREES,
JUDY MOWATT AND
RITA MARLEY

RUNNING AWAY

One of the most simple and most powerful of Marley's songs, 'Running Away', said to be written about his 18 months in exile, can be interpreted on many different levels. Of the shooting, Marley would say (in February, 1978) that he "knew something was going to happen". He had, he said, a "vision" (prophetic dream) of being in a barrage of gunshot". Knowing when he woke up that this premonition was serious, he talked about it with his "bredren", mentioning that the message of his vision was that he shouldn't run. When vision became reality and he heard the first gunshots at 56 Hope Road, his first thought was to run but, flashing back to the dream, he remembered that "in vision me nah run, so me hafe stay and not run".

Not fleeing from the gunfire saved his life. But by leaving the island shortly thereafter, first for Nassau and then for London, he was still running, living, in a sense, like his would-be murderers, on the lam. He realized then that the one impenetrable obstacle to real escape—whether from actions or feared consequences—was one's self.

CRISIS

Marley's fatalistic belief of "I knew I was born with a price on my head," gave his music much of its edge. He had just completed the recording of 'Crisis' before traveling back to a country that, in the wake of Michael Manley's misguided courting of Cuba, was facing the worst crisis in its history. The politicians plan of divide and plunder, which had worked so well for so long was now backfiring big-time as the people started to march to the radical Rasta drummer, and the downtown dons were uniting in a common people's cause. Tellingly, the PNP's minister of national security (called in the current crisis the "minister of national insecurity") denounced the peace effort.

The event that precipitated the peace initiative was the Green Bay Massacre, when ten JLP gang members were shot by the Army. Five men died. Five survived and escaped. Some thought that Manley had set it up. Others accused Seaga. But whoever was behind the slaughter, the clear message to the rival gangs was that they were all expendable pawns in the game.

This was the changing order Marley came back to. In the 'Crisis' mix, Chris Blackwell and Robert Ash captured the tension of those dangerous days, the instruments, at times, hovering like the helicopters despatched (unsuccessfully) to find the Green Bay survivors, before coming back together in the irie groove that marked the best of Marley's work. Speaking to Blackwell about this, he remembers the day that Marley did the final vocal. "I told Bob about changing 'Crisis'. There was one part that didn't work as well as the rest. He kind of grunted, but then put in a new piece instantly."

SURVIVAL

BOB MARLEY, THE
VISIONARY REGGAE
SINGER MAN

Babylon System

Ambush In The Night

Africa Unite

Top Rankin'

Wake Up And Live

Survival

Ride Natty Ride

**So Much Trouble In
The World**

Zimbabwe

Produced by: Bob Marley And
The Wailers and Alex Sadkin

1979

With a theme of African solidarity, reinforced by a Neville Garrick-designed jacket of many flags, *Survival*, the ninth of the ten albums contracted by Island Records, was released in the late summer of 1979, the Jamaican version coming out on clear vinyl with typeface in red, green and gold. Co-produced by Bob Marley And The Wailers and English engineer, Alex Sadkin (who would die in a Caribbean car accident a few years later), the album was recorded in London at Island's Basing Street Studio.

In Jamaica, things were dread. The economy had come to a standstill and the country was bankrupt. Michael Manley's vision had failed and he was now being seen as more sinner than saviour (even by some of the party's most loyal stalwarts). People began to predict that Manley would lose in the following year's election (which he did). Twenty years later, after the death of both Manley and Marley, history would repeat itself and the same party would do the same thing to the country, but that situation is still waiting for its resolution.

Despite attempts to portray him as a PNP supporter, Robert Nesta befriended the "top rankin'" of both parties, and would never acknowledge any affiliation to anything other than the "Rastafarian party". As he expressed it: "Only one government me love, the government of Rastafari."

Marley had far less difficulty aligning himself with political causes overseas, and accepted eagerly when invited to perform at the midnight ceremony held at Rufano Stadium in Salisbury (soon to be Harare) to mark the handing over of Rhodesia by the British to the Africans as the new state of Zimbabwe on April 18, 1980. "Natty gonna mash it inna Zimbabwe," he sang. And he did. Thousands of Africans wildly cheered the slight figure on as he delivered his tribute to the newly-liberated nation.

'Zimbabwe', the song that defined the independence celebration (and which appears on the *Survival* album), was not, as is commonly thought, written for the occasion. Rather, it was composed the year before in Shashamani, Ethiopia, on Marley's first visit to the African continent. Shashamani is a Rastafarian settlement built by the first (and almost the last) of the Jamaican Rastas who emigrated to Ethiopia not only believing that the ultimate goal of all Selassie I's followers was repatriation to the homeland, but having the pioneering courage to act on their belief.

Not only 'Zimbabwe' but several of the other songs on *Survival* had their origins in Shashamani. As early as 1974, Marley had verbalized his desire to "go to Africa and write some music", and when he finally "reached"— after, according to Don Taylor who was with him, two unexplained denials of his visa application by Ethiopian officials, before a third accompanied by cash was successful—the creativity flowed almost non-stop.

Co-producer Alex Sadkin, who had first worked with Bob Marley as an engineer on *Rastaman Vibration*, had been hired for the *Survival* sessions by Chris Blackwell. Although, in an interview, manager Don Taylor dismisses Sadkin as "one of Chris Blackwell's white flunkies", he describes him in his book, *Marley And Me*, as a Bob Marley find who was later lured into the Island fold. But, however he came to be involved, Alex Sadkin has always had a good reputation in reggae circles and is recognized as a legitimate contributor to the music and its international success. *Survival* is the only one of the ten albums recorded for Island Records that Chris Blackwell "had nothing at all to do with". Sadkin and Marley had full control of the production. Yet, it contains Blackwell's favourite song—'So Much Trouble In The World', a track he singles out for both its faultless content and production.

Survival is unusual in that it left no room at all for love songs. Its purpose was 100 per cent political, and was probably an attempt to balance the "soft" content of *Kaya*, and to silence the hardcore critics of his last studio album.

The title of the album spoke not only of his own narrow escape from death, and to the reversal of the black Diaspora, but would also find a resonance back home where the basic survival of the people of Jamaica into the next decade was in grave jeopardy. Supermarket shelves were bare, candles were a common option to a patchy supply of electricity, and cheques written by the government to pay the nation's bills were bouncing with alarming regularity. Manley's sweet socialist dream had now turned into a bitter nightmare of mammoth proportions.

In July of 1979, Bob Marley And The Wailers were booked to headline Reggae Sunsplash, the second year

> **"In a world that forces lifelong insecurity... all together now... we're the survivors"**
>
> **– Bob Marley**

ZIMBABWEANS TOOK
TO THE STREETS TO
CELEBRATE THEIR
INDEPENDENCE IN
1980—BOB MARLEY
PERFORMED AT THE
MIDNIGHT CEREMONY

of a festival started in Kingston that grew in a new venue in Montego Bay to be one of the biggest events in the reggae year until a string of bad business decisions resulted in the collapse of the original format and the demise of the Sunsplash vibe. The thousands of reggae addicts who would make the annual trek from places as far away as Japan and Siberia come no more, and the parks that once resounded to the driving drum and bass beat for four days and nights are now silent. No more all-night sessions of some of the best reggae music, no more complaining about long band changes, or of the bathroom attendants charging JA$1 per sheet of toilet paper. No more trying to sleep under the stage on "reggae beds" (sheets of cardboard that were sold for JA$50), and no more staggering home and feeling like you wanted to sleep for a week. But then going back and doing it all over the following year.

The night that Bob Marley and his band did the gig, it had been raining, and Sunsplash when it rained was a nightmare of mud, in parts six inches deep. In those days there were no changing rooms for artists, or even a decent shelter backstage. The routine was that the artists would arrive in minibuses, pull up to the side of the stage, and when announced, run up the high wooden stairs and straight into the spotlight. On this particular night, the mud was so bad it had even made it onto the stage and Marley joked about it as he launched into 'Lively Up Yourself', before previewing a couple of songs from *Survival*. As a continuous spiral of suspicious smoke drifted high above the crowd of 15,000, and moved slowly across the lights beamed from the back of the park, no one remembered the rain or the mud any more. Marley was burnin' "on the box"—nothing else mattered.

In September, Marley did another show in Jamaica— this one at Kingston's National Arena, a benefit for children. Again, he tried out a couple of his new tunes, but for the children, the fun started when he sang the songs that every child in Jamaica could sing the chorus to.

It was hard for Marley to stay in Jamaica during the long dark days of the late Seventies. People were selling out and leaving the island by the thousands, choosing the uncertainty of a new country and the difficulties imposed by the US$50 limit on funds that could be taken with them (all additional funds had to be left in the island), over the known hardship of Jamaica where the luxury houses they were leaving behind were fetching US$30,000 at best. A bumper sticker popular at the time read, "Will the last person to leave Jamaica please turn off the lights."

Ironically, by the end of 1979, every one of the political heavyweights who had been involved in the peace truce of the preceding year was dead. Claudie Massop and Bucky Marshall were gunned down, and Byah Mitchell died from a cocaine overdose.

> ## "Now I know I can live"
> **– Bob Marley**

BABYLON SYSTEM

In its widest interpretation, "Babylon" is the world system (or "Shitstem" as Peter Tosh called it) of inequality and injustice. In its narrowest sense it is "the vampire sucking the blood of the sufferah"—the Jamaican police. The Jamaican Constabulary Force has never had the trust or respect of the island's people, especially not that of the poor whose basic human rights have too often been blatantly ignored. Intimidated and abused (and sometimes, reportedly, even killed) more than they have been "served and protected", it is not hard to understand their reluctance to trust. With this "us" against "them" tradition, Bob Marley's words found thousands of ready ears. Everyone in the ghetto, and more than a few of his uptown followers, were willing to fight to right the wrongs of Babylon.

"Babylon is everywhere. You have wrong, and you have right. Wrong is what we call Babylon…" said Marley, who liked to boast of his ability to explain things in terms simple enough for a baby to understand, and who saw his own birth to a "white man of war" (as he once described his father) and a simple, unsullied, black country lass, as a personal example of Babylon's reach. He also cautioned against the indiscriminate use of the term by those who didn't properly understand it, explaining that, "a certain word can hold you out from the truth a long while…so (you) become an idiot (you) become more chained, 'cause a thing is right or wrong…if you're right you're right an' if you're wrong you're wrong"—put more metaphorically in the song as "you've been trodding on the wine press much too long". He had a simple answer: "Babylon no wan' peace. Babylon wan' power."

One of the key weapons of Marley's war against the wrongs of Babylon, and one of the most popular of his ideas, was the smoking of herb as the answer to, if not everything, at least a great deal. "The more people smoke herb, the more Babylon fall," he promised. Rasta promoted weed as the "healing of the nation", but also as the conveyer of truth to troubled, rebellious minds. To ensure his own access to the "truth", Marley, says Don Taylor, was the only rock star to have the "provision and supply of marijuana written into his contracts".

AMBUSH IN THE NIGHT

After the night ambush in December, 1976, Bob Marley left Jamaica in a chartered jet for the Bahamas and went into hiding for several weeks at Chris Blackwell's house in Nassau, before touring up in London to start work on the *Exodus* album in early 1977. He would not return to Jamaica until February, 1978.

His assailants, Marley said, were known to him, adding that their identity was "top secret". Although his attackers were never brought to legal justice, three of the gunmen, says Don Taylor, got stark and swift ghetto justice in June, 1978, when he and Bob were summoned as "witnesses for the prosecution" and taken to a lonely spot by the McGregor gully. He then recounts how one of the three confessed to being trained as an agent by the CIA and given unlimited supplies of guns and cocaine to ensure their cooperation in carrying out orders to kill the man who was being increasingly seen as a threat by those who had a vested interest in keeping the political "runnings" just the way they were.

The gunmen pleaded for mercy but to no avail. Two were taken away and hanged. The third was shot in the head. A fourth suspect, never apprehended by either justice system, was said to have self-destructed on cocaine. The most compelling part of Taylor's story is his description of how a "ghetto general" offered the gun to Marley, giving him the chance to personally execute his enemy. "Marley," says Taylor, with no hint of emotion, "declined the offer."

Ultimately, Marley's take on the Hope Road shooting was that it was a "good" experience, "nobody died".

AFRICA UNITE

Reggae's Messiah stated on many occasions that his message was for the whole world, but his heart was in Africa. More than anything, he said, his dream would be realized with the reunification of the separated states of his ancestral homeland. Nearly 20 years after his death, it is Europe that has united, and, apart from a slowly-growing recognition of commonality between US and Caribbean blacks, Africa and its peoples are as divided as ever.

One of the most frustrating ironies for Marley was that despite his work's Afrocentric focus, it was the white people of the world who were his first followers, and who took his cry for one love, one heart, as a call for unity and understanding within the human race. Blacks, particularly in the US were very slow to respond to reggae, and Bob Marley And The Wailers concerts drew crowds that were 85 per cent caucasian. In an effort to increase his acceptance in the black community, the rebel voice of Jamaica purposely planned that the US leg of the *Survival* tour would open at Harlem's legendary R&B venue, the Apollo Theatre.

To a degree, the ploy worked. The Apollo show was a success, winning a few more converts to the Marley cause, and generating lots of good press within the 'hood. But black radio would remain resistant to Marley's message, and to reggae in general. Then, as now, airtime was reserved for R&B (and, later, rap), and with the exception of a few weekly one-hour slots on some urban stations, reggae airplay was non-existent. It would never have a platform powerful enough to catch on in the ghetto, nor inspire black Americans the way it was intended.

In Africa, Bob Marley was more successful. Even though his visits to that continent were minimal, his impact was quite remarkable.

'Africa Unite' is Family Man Barrett's favourite Wailers' track. "Yeah," he reflects in the slow, measured delivery common to many a Rastaman, "how good and how pleasant it will be before God and man, yeah, to see the unification of all Africans."

> "How good it will be to see all Africans unite"
> — **Family Man Barrett**

TOP RANKIN'

The "top rankin'" in Jamaica are those in control. Usually, the term is used to describe the "dons" of the downtown areas who are divided according to political affiliation, but in the song the reference is clearly to the leaders of Jamaica's political parties, Michael "Joshua" Manley and Edward Seaga.

Divide and control is the political strategy that has governed Jamaica for the past several decades. Like a political patchwork quilt, downtown Kingston is made up of adjoining PNP and JLP zones, each one controlled by its own ghetto government and kept in order by party-issued guns. It is a system that worked well for those in power for many years, and though it has long been common knowledge that the politically-engineered "wars" between rival factions have greatly damaged Jamaica as a nation, no serious attempt has ever been made to stop them, and no artist since Bob Marley has consistently railed against it. "Government sometimes don't like what we say because what we say is too plain," said Marley, well aware of the potential pitfalls of speaking out.

As one who saw how it worked from within (that is, from the PNP-controlled Trench Town), and who was perceptive enough to see through the pretense of the

REGGAE'S MESSIAH PERFORMING ONE OF HIS MOST POLITICAL— AND PASSIONATE— SONGS, THE ROUSING 'AFRICA UNITE' politicians, Robert Nesta Marley's increasing popularity with the people, and the street power of words like "they don't want to see us unite, 'cause all they want us to do is keep on fussing and fighting, I tell you all they want us to do is keep on killing one another", made him a frightening threat to the political and social status quo. "I know I was born with a price on my head," he would say later.

In 1980, the year after 'Top Rankin' was released, there were 800-plus murders. It would go down in this Caribbean nation's history as its most violent to date, a record unbroken until 1998 when over 950 killings occurred. In the intervening 18 years things have changed, but not in a way that anyone—even Bob Marley—could have foreseen. Today, the ghetto dons that once were "employees" of the company, now own it, and the guns that used to be fired by order for political leverage, are now fired in far more self-serving ways. Crossing all of the old political borders, the criminals have brought unity to the communities in a way that puts the future of Kingston—and the island itself—under a very large question mark.

WAKE UP AND LIVE

Never a material man, Bob Marley, according to just about everyone who knew him, practised what he preached. His passionate plea to the people of Jamaica, not to take more than you need from society—not to live for today—has, with hindsight, been interpreted by some of his peers as a self-fulfilling prophecy, since the reasoning behind it was that "tomorrow you (might) bury inna casket". What he's saying in this song is that the only way to protect one's life in Jamaica, is to proceed with caution, and with both eyes fully open.

A recurring theme throughout the *Survival* album, and one that was certainly a natural outcome of the Hope Road shooting, is that of the necessity of losing fantasy and finding—or facing—reality.

The island of Jamaica is a place where fantasy is promoted as reality, and the paradise of the pampered few co-exists with the hell of the many. It is also a place where danger lurks around every mountain curve, and every hypocrite's smile, and what you see is never, ever what you get.

MICHAEL MANLEY, WHOSE ACTIONS IN OFFICE DIDN'T MATCH THE IDEALS THAT GOT HIM ELECTED

SURVIVAL

The album's title track, written from the vantage point of another far less troubled Caribbean island, during his brief exile in Nassau, speaks the truth about a government that bills itself as the "people's party", yet does nothing to stop the suffering endemic to the island's poor. If the government cared, the people wouldn't suffer, sings Marley, convincingly, before intimating in the chorus that black is synonymous with survival.

Part of the euphoria generated in the 1976 election came from the Michael Manley's promise to the Jamaican people of a future of self-determination, free at last of

both its colonial past, and its latter-day economic dependence on the US. Jamaica for Jamaicans was how it was sold and, for a brief time, as long as passionate theory didn't have to be backed up by practice, it worked.

Soon, however, the light offered by the people's saviour was dimmed by a dark cloud that covered the island in an unrelenting grip of desperation and hopelessness.

Interviewed in London, Marley reaffirmed his distaste for discussing Jamaica (he had previously expressed concern that doing so could lead to his arrest for treason on his return), but maintained his independent stance, and his commitment to only one political entity—Rasta, and one social goal—"to kill the system".

But, even without outside assistance the system was killing itself. In 1979, even a loaf of bread was hard to come by, each arrival of the bakery truck bringing with it hordes of people begging for their daily bread. And no one was helping. An ill-advised liaison with Cuba had guaranteed that Manley would be ostracized by the US and would be last in line for IMF handouts.

RIDE NATTY RIDE

One of the most enduring images of Rastafari's early days when the whole world seemed bathed in a red, gold and green glow, is that of a free-spirited dread, locks loose and flowing in the wind, sitting astride a high-powered motor cycle, zipping recklessly in and out of heavy Kingston traffic. Alternately, there was the rich Rastaman (by then no longer a contradiction in terms) behind the wheel of a new, black, well-polished BMW (which Marley only bought, he said, because it stood for Bob Marley And The Wailers). Either take was a striking visual reminder of Rasta the rebel, the promise-keeper of the poor, and the bearer of hope for a more righteous and more prosperous tomorrow.

"Natty Dread" is a slang term for any male who sports dreadlocks, "natty" referring to knotted locks, and "dread" being either a real Rastaman or someone who wears locks only for style. The natty dread of the song is Bob, riding on "no matter what they do… or say". He talks of his survival and, in a broader interpretation, the survival of the Rastaman against the formidable odds of

almost total societal rejection. The song ends with what is probably a reference to the fiery destruction of the infamous Jamaican city of Port Royal (known in 1692, the year it disappeared beneath the Caribbean Sea in a fiery ball after a massive earthquake, as the wickedest city on earth), that could be construed as equally applicable to Kingston in the twentieth century, and Rasta's apocalyptic vision of its eventual demise.

Rasta the rebel, the promise-keeper of the poor, and the bearer of hope for a more righteous tomorrow

CHRIS BLACKWELL ON THE PATIO OF HIS COTTAGE ON THE HILL IN OCHO RIOS IN THE MID-EIGHTIES. LIKE MARLEY, CHRIS FAVOURS CASUAL CLOTHES AND, IN JAMAICA, IS RARELY SEEN IN ANYTHING OTHER THAN T-SHIRT AND SHORTS

SO MUCH TROUBLE IN THE WORLD

The word "illusion" appears more than once in the lyrics of *Survival*'s songs. This, coupled with directives like "wake up and live" indicate a deep inner struggle with the widening gap between reality and the fantasy that the decadence of the Studio 54 scenes of the Seventies—all of which had made it down to Jamaica—would make the pain go away. A "million miles from reality", Marley muses. And everyone was. People found it easier to disco the night away than to deal with the truth that morning light revealed. Having survived an attempt on his life, Bob Marley was more than aware of what the real world was about, but he also knew from that experience what survival was all about, too.

In some parts of Jamaica—where shops sell T-shirts emblazoned with the slogan, "Jamaica No Problem"—it is easy to believe the fantasy of the trouble-free tropical island where pleasure never co-exists with pain. The northcoast hotels, many of which exclude any local who doesn't drive a "Bimmer" or a "Benz", promote the tourist dream of never-ending fun amid pretty green palm trees and white sand beaches. The first of the all-inclusive hotels, where real life stops at the security gate, opened in Ocho Rios in 1978, the same year that *Survival* came out.

In contrast to all this pretense, Rastafari *was* reality. And as its primary spokesman, Marley's mission was to open the eyes of the blind and the ears of the deaf and show them that the only way forward was not to run from trouble, nor hide from the truth, but to face it head on and deal with it. "'Cause first thing," he said, "you cannot be ignorant."

When Chris Blackwell is asked why 'So Much Trouble' is his favourite song, he says, "Because it's a perfect track—the mix, sound, vocal, lyrics and melody are all superb."

> ## "'So Much Trouble' is a perfect track—mix, vocal, lyrics are all superb"
> ### – Chris Blackwell

PRINCE CHARLES INFORMALLY GREETS CROWDS AT THE HIGHFIELD TOWNSHIP, ZIMBABWE, FOLLOWING INDEPENDENCE

ZIMBABWE

Dressed in tight black leather pants and matching vest, Marley sang this song of liberation before a sea of beaming, bopping Zimbabweans, who knowing all the words, sang along with their hero. The decision to appear at the independence celebration had been made spontaneously, and confirmed only a couple of days before its date. Expenses for the trip were borne not by the new government, but by Bob Marley himself, and Denise Mills, Chris Blackwell's long-time PA and

confidante, and a woman who could "get through" with anything once she made up her mind to do so, arranged everything (on Bob's orders) from London in, she said in one of her rare conversations about Bob, "only two days". On the Sunday before the Tuesday of the show, Mills joined Bob's entourage when, after coming in from the heat of Kingston that morning, they left London's Heathrow airport on a regularly scheduled BA flight bound for Harare and an official government welcome. For Mills, as used as she was to travelling with The Wailers, the Zimbabwe visit was a surreal affair. The juxtaposition of the precise colonial manners of Rhodesia (which didn't die as quickly as its name), with the raw, rebellious zeal of liberated Zimbabwe created a circus-like atmosphere, where, as she described it, pomp and circumstance gave way to unfettered joy.

Bob Marley And The Wailers went onstage just after the new red, green and gold flag (which had got momentarily tangled at the base of the flagpole) was finally up and flying and HRH Prince Charles and President Mugabe had taken their seats for the show. The first words spoken to the newly-christened country were "Viva Zimbabwe"; the first song, 'Positive Vibration'. From the outset, the energy of the crowd was explosive and by the time Marley get to 'I Shot The Sheriff' some ten minutes later, any semblance of order was gone. The police, afraid of a riot, responded by firing tear gas into the restive crowd, whereupon The Wailers left the stage, only coming back when calm was restored.

The "Zimbabwe" sing-a-long closed the show. Marley was later to comment on how he had felt solidarity with the people. He would also imply that because the song was written the year before Zimbabwe's independence, and "when the song come out it just happen", that prophecy had played a part in it. Describing what for Marley was a momentous event, he said in an interview with journalist Stephen Davis: "We go to the ceremony to play and we watch the whole thing. Watch the British flag go down and the Zimbabwe flag go up... tell you bwoy... we hear alla dem cannon go off, about 40 yard from where we're standin', y'know. You can just imagine that and how we felt."

UPRISING

Work

Redemption Song

Forever Loving Jah

Bad Card

Real Situation

We And Them

Pimper's Paradise

Zion Train

Could You Be Loved?

Coming In From The Cold

Produced by: Bob Marley And The Wailers

MARLEY WITH JUDY MOWATT AND SOME OF THE WAILERS AFTER RECEIVING AN AWARD, CIRCA 1979

1980

It was during the recording of *Uprising* that Bob Marley started to feel that something was wrong and suspect that the minor toe injury of a few years back had turned into a major problem. But it was too late, and no one could ever have predicted that such a small axe could fell such a mighty tree.

Uprising was recorded at Dynamics, the studio owned by musician Byron Lee and, for a long time, the best in the country. Not that it was pleasant to record there. Located in a bleak and often dangerous industrial area close to the docks and to Trench Town, the studio itself, like all studios "on the rock" sits behind high, locked and security-manned gates and is only accessible to people who have business being there. Everything about Dynamics was, and remains, basic. Even in 1980, in the middle of its heyday, it offered no frills. But The Wailers, as always, were flexible, and as long as the sound was right (Dynamics could deliver that) and the smoke plentiful, "tings aright".

On January 1, 1980, Bob Marley And The Wailers played their first live gig in Africa. The country was Gabon. The occasion, a birthday party for the president. This performance, apart from being The Wailers' African debut, was significant in a couple of ways. First, Marley met the president's daughter, Pascaline, a woman he was to woo and conquer and with whom he had one of his last serious affairs. And, second, a dispute over monies paid for the show—Marley reportedly only got $40,000 of a reputed $60,000 fee—led to a parting of the ways with manager Don Taylor. Taylor insists that he did nothing wrong, that "any such accusation was unfounded", and cites as proof of his client's ongoing trust the fact that the majority of Bob's assets "remained in my name until after his death". Even so, he lost his post as manager, an opening soon claimed jointly by Skill Cole and Marley's former manager, Danny Sims.

Back in Jamaica, in February, Bob Marley and his band finished most of the overdubbing on the tracks recorded for *Uprising,* following which Marley took the one-hour 15-minute flight from Jamdown to visit his mother in Miami, and to cool out for a couple of weeks before going on to Rio for a five-day trip.

While in Brazil, Marley's health was reportedly good and his writing prolific. But two days after he returned to Jamaica, Inner Circle's lead singer, Jacob Millar, who, with Junior Marvin had gone on the Rio trip with Bob, was killed in a car accident in New Kingston, an event that affected Marley deeply.

When, in April, 1980, Bob Marley And The Wailers got the headline spot at the Zimbabwean independence celebrations, it was, remembered Denise Mills, at very short notice. Against great odds she got Bob, the band and the equipment from points A and B to C on time, but it was "all a bit bizarre". After an official government welcome, the kind normally reserved for heads of state, and an afternoon courtesy call on President Mugabe at the palace (replete with an acoustic offering of 'No Woman No Cry' by the guest of honour at the palace piano), the actual performance was interrupted by rioting fans (the ones that weren't allowed in).

Tear gas and the Zimbabwe National Liberation Army guerrillas restored order. A second concert was hurriedly arranged for the following night to placate the people, uncounted thousands of whom showed up for the event. Mills, on the surface a rather conventional Englishwoman who lived a very unconventional life, and who was never phased by the worst of problems, rated the trip to Zimbabwe as "very difficult". Though Marley was pleased that he'd helped the new country usher in its future, "everyone", she said "was glad to go home".

By May, *Uprising* had been mixed and what would be The Wailers' last European tour began in Austria. This time around, the band was playing the big venues, like the San Siro Stadium in Milan, Italy. Several of those on the tour speak of the Milan show as the most inspiring that The Wailers ever did. Engineer Errol Browne, who with Dennis Thomson, was responsible for the sound on the tour, did both the Zimbabwe and the Milan shows and says that the sheer number of people that showed up for the latter concert was, in 1980, astounding. "Not even football had drawn so many people," he said of the 100,000 who attended. Browne also recalls that the Average White Band was the opening act, and that the audience started throwing eggs at them: "They wanted Bob."

Neville Garrick, Marley's art director who designed most of the Wailers' album covers and all of the stage

> "I got a pain in my throat and head and it's killin' me... I've nevah felt this way before in mi life"
> **– Bob Marley**

backdrops, watched the Milan concert from atop 20ft speakers, and remembers that "when Bob came onstage the whole place shook".

Three thousand miles away, Jamaicans were shaking, too, as the country entered the longest, hottest summer in its history. By the end of 1980, the death toll from election-related violence would be estimated at 750, and the new prime minister, Edward Seaga (or CIAga as he would become known) would inherit a country that was in a shambles.

When a visibly-exhausted Robert Marley returned to London for a short break before the tour was due to fly west for the mid-September start of the North American dates, he briefly considered a return to Jamaica with his bandmates, but in the end, heeded a warning that he might once again be a target and, after a couple of weeks playing soccer, went to Miami instead. His health was deteriorating daily. "I got a pain in my throat and head and it's killin' me. It's like somebody… is tryin' to kill me. I feel like I've been poisoned… and somethin' wrong wid me voice. I've nevah felt this way before in mi life."

As the tenth album recorded for Island Records, and the end of his commitment to the label, *Uprising* was, says Blackwell, "the most simple of them all". His strategy to market The Wailers as a pop act had worked, and the label head now wanted The Wailers' fans to come to reggae instead of adapting the music to suit them. On first hearing the completed album, he thought they needed two uptempo tunes to balance the overall feel of the album. As always, Marley was accommodating—"Bob was always humble enough to accept advice," is how Errol Browne describes him—and came back in a couple of days with two of the best songs on the album: 'Could You Be Loved?' and 'Coming In From The Cold'. "He'd probably had them for ages," speculates Blackwell, who was now satisfied that *Uprising* was ready for release. The first single, 'Could You Be Loved?' was an instant hit on both sides of the Atlantic.

Boston had been the first US city to catch on to Bob Marley And The Wailers, and it was a fitting place to kick off the US leg of the band's last tour. As ever, Boston fans

JACOB MILLAR
OF INNER CIRCLE,
LONDON, 1979—
HE WAS KILLED IN
A KINGSTON CAR
ACCIDENT IN 1980

gave the pre-eminent Jamaican band a great Irish welcome and spirits were high as the tour buses headed south to New York City and a two-night booking at Madison Square Gardens as co-headliners with The Commodores. For Errol Browne, the first night at the Gardens was one of the few he remembers as nerve-wracking. "There had been no sound check," he says, "and we were all nervous. But," he adds, "somehow it all came together."

It came together so well for Bob, and his band bredren, confides Browne, that The Commodores threatened to pull Bob offstage and pull the plug. Warming up to the story, he continues: "Lionel Richie was singing 'All Night Long', but the crowd wasn't into it at all. But for 'Could You Be Loved?', the whole place broke down."

> ## "Bob was always humble enough to accept advice"
> **– Errol Browne, engineer**

The day after the second show, the man who once again had upstaged a major act, himself broke down during a short jog in Central Park. Initiated by Skill Cole in an attempt to combat Marley's growing lethargy, the plan backfired when The Skip collapsed and had to be helped back through the park and across the street to his regular New York hotel, the Essex. There, the stark gravity of Marley's illness would finally begin to sink in.

At the Essex, a high-class hotel with a high tolerance for unorthodox guests, the relatively innocuous ganja smoking that had always surrounded Marley and his entourage had given way to a far more ominous scene. At about the same time as cocaine was finding its way (with a little help from some influential friends) into Jamaica, and seeping into (and eventually almost destroying) the naive and vulnerable Rasta camps back home, it had infiltrated Bob Marley's portable world to the point where hard drugs were as much a part of reggae as they were of rock.

To the then 13-year-old Junior Tucker, the blatant use of coke made a disturbing impression. Recalling a scene in a New York nightclub, he tells of Marley and a couple of radio people "hanging out and doing coke right there in the open with four models… Bob was acting like he was possessed… he was cussing everyone, his eyes were red and he looked evil… he'd moved from humble street person to raging rock star." This was the reality of the

THE COMMODORES, HAMMERSMITH, LONDON, 1979: UPSTAGED BY THE WAILERS IN NYC

reggae king's last days on the road. Although the tour continued on to Pittsburgh where, on September 23, 1980, the final Bob Marley And The Wailers show was performed, it was obvious that the Gong could go no further. The Wailers' PR people called all the writers who had interviews arranged to tell them that Marley was fighting exhaustion and was taking a few days off. The official story was that he was going to stay with his mother, to get some good home cooking, and that the tour would soon pick up in Toronto. The interviews would, the writers were assured, be rescheduled. But they never were. The last song performed, in Pittsburgh, was 'Work'.

WORK

Fairly or not, the average Jamaican "born a ghetto" is often accused by the country's middle class of having a "freeness" mentality, of wanting what someone else has without working for it. Rastas, on the other hand, of any class origin, have always, like the proverbial Friday's child, worked hard for a living. With the exception of rent-a-dreads, the "Rasta imposters" who attach themselves, parasite-like, to gullible and usually generous white women, members of the Rastafari faith have a strict work ethic and a strong belief in self-sufficiency. Whether it be music or any other creative pursuit, a true Rastaman is seldom idle, and generally focuses on doing as much of the "Father's work" as possible.

This song rallies the troops and in the fashion of the eighteenth and nineteenth century work songs that got slaves through long hot days of toil on sugar plantations, imparts the message that teamwork not only gets the job done, but provides emotional support as well.

Marley himself was always open to team input. While no one was ever allowed to forget that the Gong ruled, his openness to good ideas is cited by many of his musical intimates. "There are some Jamaican artists who can't be told anything," says an engineer at Anchor Recording Studio, who prefers—because he has named the difficult ones—to talk anonymously. "But Bob Marley was never like that. He was just cool to work with."

> ## "Bob Marley was never like that [difficult]. He was just cool to work with"
>
> **– anonymous engineer**

REDEMPTION SONG

The venue is Jarrett Park, Montego Bay, August, 1981, at about 3:00am. Stevie Wonder is onstage at Reggae Sunsplash with Rita Marley, Third World and other Jamaican musicians, paying homage to Robert Nesta Marley.

A crowd of 10,000 people of every color, creed, class and country join Stevie in saluting their fallen hero. The Master Blaster is no longer jammin', and already, only a few months after his departure, he is sorely missed.

The most moving moments of the remembrance belong to Dean Fraser who, with his horn, plays a version of 'Redemption Song' (the final track on *Uprising*) that cuts through the early morning air and silences the entire park. Not a sound disturbs the music. And not a person present will ever forget Fraser's farewell to Bob.

Often cited as the work that most expresses the mind of Bob Marley, 'Redemption Song' illustrates the complexity of that mind and its often contradictory path. On an album where he says, "seems like total destruction the only solution", he also says—on 'Redemption Song' itself—"Have no fear for atomic energy, 'cos none of them can stop the tide", and that this line was meant for those who would "put the fear into mankind that everything must be destroyed... me say, 'have no fear' ca' man mus' have hope'".

'Redemption Song' was originally recorded with full musical backing. Many people claim credit for the

original idea of an acoustic version (including Cindy Breakespeare who says that Bob, in answer to her oft-asked question of why he didn't do an acoustic version, responded, "me is not a big singer like Luther Vandross"), but credit for the recording of an acoustic rendition is given by Errol Browne to Chris Blackwell.

"Blackwell had great input on 'Redemption Song'. It was recorded over and over, and then one day Blackwell walked in and called over to Bob and said, 'I want to hear this with you alone with the guitar,' and he didn't argue.

"He just did it and it sounded great."

FOREVER LOVING JAH

Reason with any Rastaman and at some point in the conversation he will refer, as Marley does in this song, to the Biblical revelation that what is hidden from the wise and prudent is revealed to the babe and suckling. As Errol Browne observes, "Bob's lyrics got more serious after the shooting," but this song, said to have been written about that traumatic incident, tempers the still painful memories with the joyful discovery that "we've found a way to cast away the fears, forever, yeah", which then leads into the catchy, sing-a-long chorus about forever loving Jah, and the acceptance in the final verse that "everything in life got its purpose".

Pledging his allegiance to Jah in this song (as he also did before beginning his live performances with the call and response "Jah", "Rastafari"), Marley could never have imagined that one day 100,000 white people in Milan would sing along with him word for word.

'Forever Loving Jah' was Carly Barrett's favourite song. Barrett—who was murdered allegedly by his wife and her lover in Kingston in 1987—was, like brother Family Man, a diehard reggae traditionalist, and as the drummer for The Wailers, was the anchor of a rhythm so close to the root it never sounds stale. As Sly Dunbar is fond of saying: "It all starts with the drum."

BAD CARD

'Bad Card' was written at Hope Road. Cindy Breakespeare remembers that the night it was recorded Bob came by her house with a cassette— "He used to call me late at night, about 12:30, and say, 'What a gwan?' (what's happening) and then come over." On this night he put the cassette into her portable player ("the ones that were popular at the time") and danced around the room saying how "it sweet him".

Junior Tucker was at the old white mansion on Hope Road the night the song was created. He remembers the neighbours complaining about the noise (a regular occurrence at the Marley residence). "They were cussing him from across the street," Tucker relates. "The police came three times and Bob didn't care." With The Wailers looking on, "He sat in the front yard looking at the people and wrote the song and then turned up the speakers and started singing it."

Marley also warns his enemies in the wider society, who by 1980 numbered many, that they "a go tired fi see mi face", not having an inkling at the time just how tired they would be. Breakespeare points out that Bob "liked using catch phrases and 'bad card' was popular at the time". In Jamaica, to "draw" a bad card means someone is out to get you. Another interpretation has it that the song was about Don Taylor's apparent betrayal, but Marley fell out with Taylor in January, 1980, at a time when *Uprising* was said to have been finished. Marley was pleased when "someone call me from Jamaica and tell me one political party is using 'Bad Card'. Music is music. It heal de scar."

REAL SITUATION

One of Marley's most quoted lines, especially in times of what Jamaican broadcasters call "civil unrest", and most people call "riots", is the line from 'Real Situation' that goes "well it seems like total destruction the only solution". Used to legitimize the rampant burning and looting that usually accompanies such disputes and frequently as a warning of worse things to come, Marley's anarchistic advice may yet prove prophetic.

In the *Sunday Gleaner* of May 10, 1999, columnist Dawn Rich, known for outspoken and unvarnished socio-political commentary, referred to Jamaica's recent gas riots as only the beginning of what could be a full-scale insurrection if the Patterson government continues to ignore the people's plight. As Bob said: "No one can stop them now."

In Marley's day there was more of a balance between reason and "bruk out", and, despite Marley's dire prediction, order probably would have prevailed.

Today, the response of the people to all perceived or real injustices is so swift there is no time for reason, and small chance of stopping them.

WE AND THEM

There were many parallels between the North American hippies of the Sixties and the small Caribbean cult that transformed itself into a global force of surprising strength. Both hippies and Rastas were motivated by music and both promoted a then radical philosophy of peace and love, both favouring the open marketing of marijuana, and both paying homage to the sanctity of Mother Earth. Then came the disco-dominated Seventies during which most of the hippies got jobs and went straight. The Rastas just got more militant and it was left to them to carry the message forward. "We and them"—the Rasta and the shitstem—unlikely, as reggae's militant Messiah saw it, ever to "work it out".

> **"It seems like total destruction the only solution"**
>
> **– Bob Marley**

PIMPER'S PARADISE

Don Taylor's version of this song is that "it tells the story of the women in Bob's life… including Rita Marley… it's a mixture of both Cindy and Rita" (neither of whom., not surprisingly, give Taylor any credibility). A more generic interpretation endorsed by many Jamaican men is that it addresses a serious problem among young, single Jamaican women: that all they are interested in is "lookin' a boops" (a meal ticket) and a good time. And Bob Marley, perhaps the ultimate "boops", attracted his share of good-time girls.

At the time the song was penned, the righteous Rasta was rapidly being drawn to the dark and decadent side of international pop music. Though it is believed that this change began in Jamaica, on tour, The Wailers were beset upon by drug pushers who followed the rock routine described well by Def Leppard guitarist Steve Clark shortly before he died. "We'd leave a city at 2:00am, drive all night to the next stop and they'd be there waiting for us. They'd get on the bus and always had anything we wanted." Marley's appetite for willing women soon developed into what several witnesses describe as a destructive and degenerate lifestyle. Yet, immersed in it as he may have been, he never lost his acerbic eye and ability to suss out the "real situation".

ZION TRAIN

To the Rastaman, Zion is the ultimate destination. In physical terms, Africa. In metaphysical terms, heaven. One of the greatest attractions of the Rasta faith has always been its promise of a better tomorrow… its vision of peace "train", the opportunity of being saved.

And so the multitudes came to Marley, to join his "train" of redemption. And once again, although the message was aimed at the black Diaspora—"its divide and rule could only tear us apart"—whites, the most zealous with strange versions of dreadlocks and even stranger adopted names, wanted on the train, too.

As Bob Marley And The Wailers made their way around the world, the train was manifesting itself as a human chain connected by a common, globe-circling thread of red, green and gold.

> A human chain connected by a common, globe-circling thread of red, green and gold

COULD YOU BE LOVED?

What appears to be a love song really isn't. After the first two lines, the lyrics take a philosophical twist and the song becomes a standard Marley commentary on the ills of Babylon, complete with a series of familiar (almost hackneyed) adages to make his point.

One of the two songs pulled from Marley at the last minute when Chris Blackwell asked for two uptempo songs to "balance the feel of the album", 'Could You Be Loved?' appealed to black Americans more than any previous Wailers tune and increased the group's presence in that market substantially by being added to urban stations that had long been resistant to reggae (and which would continue to be so after Marley's death). Many of these listeners, used as they were to much lighter fare, may have missed the full message, but the music was at last getting through.

COMING IN FROM THE COLD

Said to have been written in Miami, 'Coming In From The Cold' speaks, on a superficial level, to all who are familiar with the joyous feeling of stepping off the plane after landing back in Jamaica from somewhere cold, and feeling that first blast of hot, tropical air on your face that tells you you're home. But, beyond that, it makes a personalized plea—"It's you I'm talking to now"—to those not yet committed to the fight for equal rights and justice to "come in".

This was the second uptempo number that Chris Blackwell received to round out an album that, as

it stood, he felt, mixed the militant with too much mellow.

Most remarkable about 'Coming In From The Cold' and 'Could You Be Loved?' is the driving energy in the rhythm. Engineer Sylvan Morris, who did a lot of work with The Wailers at Harry J's, and who still works at Dynamics, felt that the band's music took a commercial turn from *Kaya* onward.

"The earlier albums seemed to have more drive," he has said. But it is hard to imagine songs with more of a drive than these last two cuts to make the *Uprising* LP.

CONFRONTATION

Give Thanks And Praise

Jump Nyabinghi

Chant Down Babylon

Trench Town

I know

Blackman Redemption

Mix Up Mix Up

Stiff Necked Fools

Buffalo Soldier

Produced by: Chris Blackwell and Rita Marley

1983

"Bob Marley is exhausted," said the female caller. "The tour is being delayed a few weeks so that he can get some rest at his mother's house in Miami." It was a cleverly constructed story told with an air of sharing a confidence. No journalist who got such a call from Howard Bloom's PR staff thought the situation to be serious, and those affected were assured that all interviews would soon be rescheduled. But they never were.

Marley did fly to Miami, staying with his mother for a few days before returning to New York for more tests. "He looked tired and drawn," his mother recalls.

Back in New York, Marley entered New York's respected Sloan Kettering Hospital, where he was expected to stay for several weeks. But when word of the hospital's famous patient leaked to the media, and the tabloids got hold of the story, Bob checked out and went to stay at a friend's apartment (although another version has it that his doctors at Sloan Kettering said they could do nothing further for him, and that he was discharged). But in either event, a short while after he left the hospital, Mrs Booker received a call saying that her son wanted to see her. On arrival, she heard that Nesta had an inoperable brain tumour and that, without treatment, he had a life expectancy of three weeks.

After sending for his trusted friend, Dr Carl ("Pee Wee") Fraser, a physician at Kingston's University Hospital, who immediately flew to New York, it was decided that Marley should go to the Issels Clinic in Bavaria. Run by Dr Josef Issels, a man who had earned some international credibility in treating terminal cancer patients, the clinic was considered the singer's only hope of survival.

But, for the tropically attuned and by now very weakened Bob Marley, Bavaria, with its long winter and generous snowfall, proved a difficult and trying place to be treated. By all accounts, he was not comfortable there, but tried gamely to cooperate with Issels and benefit as much as possible from the program.

Cindy Breakespeare says that she worried about him being there, and that personally she had favored an alternate treatment facility in Mexico that had also been considered. "It was culture shock in Germany," she says "and there was snow up to the window sill."

Other friends and family echo Cindy's feelings, but, as she sums up, "it was his decision, based on advice from those he trusted. A so he lived, a so he died."

He was kept company in this alien land by a stream of visiting "bredren", including "Skill" Cole, "Bird", a reputed Trench Town gunman turned chef, and Pee Wee. Rita Marley came and went, said Denise Mills, as did Pascaline Gabon (daughter of the president of Gabon). Marley spent his days watching Bruce Lee kung fu movies (a near-addiction for Jamaican males at that time), taking short walks, napping or reading. Rarely, he would try to write, picking gamely at his guitar.

By this time, the lion had lost his wondrous mane, a victim of the chemotherapy he had received in New York. Wife Rita would keep the lost locks and later have them woven into a wig which was placed on her husband's head for his funeral. But, in Germany, Marley kept his head covered by a Rasta tam, nursing a new growth of hair underneath.

After a few months had passed, the men (who Bob's mother called "hangers on") left Germany (some of them, according to Mrs Booker, at her insistence, after she and Rita had secretly tape-recorded one of their conversations), leaving three females to care for Bob: mother Cedella, Diane Jobson (his trusted lawyer and close friend), and Denise Mills.

Mills, a short time before her own death, recalled those days as some of the saddest and most traumatic of her life, saying that "as ill as he was, Bob never lost his spirit", nor, she said, did he lose his mental acuity. He knew what was going on and that he had a couple of traitors in his camp. He also knew that Dr Issels' treatment hadn't worked and that it was time to leave Germany. Then, surprisingly, said Mills, given the pair's acrimonious parting several years before, "he said he wanted to see Don Taylor".

Don Taylor was in LA when he got the call from Bob saying that he was leaving the Issels Clinic for Miami and wanted to meet Taylor there. During this conversation, Marley told Taylor that numerous people had been pressuring him to make a Will (a fact confirmed by Mrs Booker). "He told me that he wanted all his money to go to his children," says Taylor, "and that I should make sure they got it." Recognizing "a sense of finality" at the other end of the phone, Taylor made

> "I've been here before and will come again"
>
> **– Bob Marley**

MARLEY TAKEN DURING THE LAST FEW MONTHS OF HIS LIFE.

plans to leave for Miami. But, he says, wondering out loud if he let Bob down, he "wouldn't quite make it in time for the meeting".

As Taylor was leaving LA, in Germany, Denise Mills was chartering a Lufthansa jet (at a cost of $90,000) to fly Marley to Miami's Cedars of Lebanon Hospital.

On Saturday, May 9, 1982, Marley, Booker, Mills and Jobson left the rented Bavarian house that had been home for the past few months, and made their way—with Bob on a gurney, attended by two doctors and a nurse, and dressed in new clothes purchased especially for the flight—to the airport and the waiting 747. Mills described the flight as "very quiet, very sad". All seven passengers on that large empty aircraft knew what fate was waiting at the end of the flight.

Two days later, on May 11, in a small, private suite at Cedars Lebanon, Robert Nesta Marley, after telling his mother not to cry, went home to Zion.

Confrontation, a title that Marley had already decided on while still working on *Uprising*, and his tenth studio album for Island, was released posthumously in 1983.

The narrow, pot-holed road that twists through the hills of the Parish of St Ann to the village of Nine Miles, where Bob Marley was born and now lies for ever, seems endless. It was 19 years ago, almost to this day of writing, that hundreds of people lined this road, a few of the hundreds of thousands who had stood, solemnly, all across the island, as Marley made his final journey from Kingston back to his birthplace. But nothing much has changed in the tiny hamlet since. In fact, says one elderly resident whose lined and weathered face appears carved from mahogany, not that much has changed since Marley's birth in 1945.

Cedella Booker, a friendly, self-assured, and outspoken Rastawoman, has built a house and a restaurant beside her son's simple, concrete mausoleum (where he lies facing to the east, and the continent of Africa). Commuting between Jamaica and Miami, Booker tries to spend as much time at Nine Miles as she can, mingling with the steady stream of visitors who make the long trek to this rural retreat from almost every place on the planet.

On this particular day, she is holding private court on a veranda talking about the plans she has for the restaurant. It is in the midst of many years of wrangling over her son's estate, and she laments the fact that the whole family hasn't come together and says that "they all forgot that it is I who laid the golden egg". She makes bitter reference to the fact that she was almost removed from the Miami house that Bob bought for her because, she maintains, Don Taylor elected to take out a low-interest mortgage and put the cash that could have bought it outright into high-return investments. It was, she confides, Chris Blackwell who came to her rescue and bought the house (not daughter-in-law, Rita). Not surprisingly, her opinion of Blackwell is high.

"He was like a big brother to Bob. Chris is like family to me—the world has to know that."

Drawing on a spliff, she adds that "Chris was ordained by the Almighty (to straighten out the estate). This is a job he must do. I don't know why everyone must fight against him."

The wrought-iron gates to the concrete crypt—which was manually constructed by local builders—are marked by a red, green and gold Rasta flag, and manned by several country dreads. In the first few years after Bob died, visitors could just hang out and "reason" with his Rasta bredren, or pay respect beside The Skip's tomb (which now also contains the body of his half-brother, Anthony, who, at 19, was, she says, shot and killed by an off-duty Miami cop), without time-limit or restriction. Now, a guided tour of the property is mandatory and costs US$10.

The tour includes the tiny, one-room house where Bob was born. Beside the small, metal, single bed, a candle burns.

A photograph of the man who spent his first, and some of his happiest years on earth in this bare, board room, and who later, with wife Rita, would come "back to country to cool out"—and no doubt share "the shelter of (the) single bed" immortalised in 'Is This Love?'—is placed next to the candle.

A short walk from the house, set high on a hill, is the mausoleum. Before entering the modest building, visitors are required to remove their shoes. Inside, the spirit of Jah's highest steppin' soldier envelops those open to its presence.

The tomb itself is covered in burlap (or "crocus" as Jamaicans call it), on which are painted, in "ites" green and gold, the symbols of Rastafari. At the base of the tomb are a variety of personal objects left as offerings by Bob's devoted fans—locks of hair, poems and tiny talismans, and Bob's first box guitar.

MARLEY'S MOTHER, CEDELLA MALCOLM MARLEY BOOKER

GIVE THANKS AND PRAISE

'Give Thanks And Praise' was written in the late Seventies when Bob Marley's Rasta faith was becoming ever more important in his life. In this song, he conveys the depth of his faith to his fans and his belief in Jah's unfailing "guidance and protection" (a common Rasta greeting).

In a New York hotel room, shortly before his death, Bob Marley became a member of the Ethiopian Orthodox Church, and part of the Christian branch of Rastafari. The Ethiopian Church embraces both Jesus and Jah, baldhead and Rasta, and finds no conflict in doing so. Established in Kingston in 1969, at the behest of a group of Rastamen, the order holds that Haile Selassie, as the direct descendant of King Solomon and the Queen of Sheba, was entitled, as the ruler of Ethiopia, to hold the titles, King of Kings, Lord of Lords, Conquering Lion of the Tribe of Judah, a

belief that concurs with Rasta doctrine. Not all Rastafarians concur with the beliefs of the Ethiopian Church, however, and Marley's baptism signalled a break with his Twelve Tribes of Israel bredren.

Ethiopian priests officiated at the May 21st, 1981 funeral of Robert Nesta Marley—as they would do in 1987 at Peter Tosh's. The priests were led by the Archbishop of the Ethiopian Church for the Western Hemisphere. The funeral service for "Berhane Selassie" (Marley's baptismal name) began at Holy Trinity church on Maxfield Avenue at 8:00am and continued at 11:00am at the National Arena, The bare, concrete hall was decorated with red, green and gold bunting, and above the similarly

> "One bright morning when my work is over, I will fly away home"
>
> **– Bob Marley**

OFFICIAL FUNERAL SERVICE OF THE LATE HON. ROBERT NESTA MARLEY O.M.

draped, temporary altar was a large banner with the words, "Hon Robert Nesta Marley, OM" (for Order of Merit, Jamaica's highest honour, which was bestowed on the musician shortly before his death). The service itself gave thanks and praise for the remarkable life of one of Jamaica's most revered sons—"It was like a jubilee," says Judy Mowatt.

Both the incumbent prime minister, Edward Seaga, and the deposed Michael Manley attended the service. Edward Seaga, paying tribute to Kingston's fallen idol, quoted the old spiritual that Marley had adapted and made his own… "One bright morning when my work is over, I will fly away home."

JUMP NYABINGHI

A Nyabingi (or Nyabinghi) is a Rastafarian gathering. A jump up is a party. Put them together and a good time is had by all. And, as the Rasta movement's unofficial leader, and as someone who knew how to enjoy himself, Marley's joyful and infectious vocal on this track comes close to explaining his timeless appeal.

The first Nyabinghi (originally called a convention) was held in Kingston's infamous ghetto area, Back O Wall, in 1958, and was scheduled to last a month. Organized as a sort of early send-off for some 300 Rastas who believed they were about to embark on a mass back-to-Africa journey (which never materialized), the event, consisting as it did of dancing, drumming and plenty of smoking around a huge bonfire of old tires, caused consternation among the city's fathers. Thereafter, Nyabinghis have been held primarily in the hills where the worship of Jah, and the celebration of the holy herb can go on (and on and on and on) undisturbed.

Reggae music lets you dance without a partner. Dancing solo is not only accepted, it is expected. Stoned dreads, skanking happily alone is a sign of a good Nyabinghi, and at reggae concerts it's quite OK to prance through the crowd, or just "hol' your corner", letting the music do with you what it will. As the drums beat, and the chillum pipe is passed through the long night, the Nyabinghi provides a communal affirmation of faith to the usually disparate and disconnected Rasta tribes.

Although not known to frequent too many Nyabinghis in the latter part of his life (time constraints alone preventing him), in the early days of his conversion to Rastafari, Bob Marley was known to have been a regular participant.

This song was, according to Island Records, a particular favourite of the singer's. The original tracks were laid down by Marley and Carly Barrett, the only two Wailers who were not temporarily felled by vaccinations (prior to The Wailers' trip to Gabon). 'Jump Nyabinghi', notable for Barrett's innovative hi-hat, was recorded along with an unreleased song, 'Jungle Fever' (referring to the vaccination, not to black/white liaisons as the phrase would later be interpreted).

RASTAFARIANS, SYMBOLIC RODS IN HAND, FACING UP TO BABYLON

CHANT DOWN BABYLON

First called 'I Believe in Reggae Music' when penned in a Belgium hotel room while The Wailers were on the *Survival* tour, 'Chant Down Babylon' starts off on a very radical note with its threat to "burn down Babylon". But then the word "burn" changes to "chant" and the suggestion of violence as a solution dissolves into a benign resolution to the problem. Music is ultimately a stronger agent of change than any other medium—the reason why Marley was such a threat to the establishment.

'Chant Down Babylon' was written for the *Uprising* album, but not included in the chosen ten. By the time it surfaced on *Confrontation*, the once esoteric terms employed to make Marley's points were finding their way into the speech of North Americans. "Babylon" had become a convenient way to describe anyone in authority. The poet of rebellion had by then been embraced not only by the avant garde of the East and West coasts, but also by by middle America.

TRENCH TOWN

Bob Marley may have physically left Trench Town, but its mark on his psyche was indelible, and the rhythm of the streets of the community he grew up in would be in his blood for ever. It was Trench Town that added the cynical edge to the sweet brown boy from Brown's Town, and what gave his music both its truth and its winning tough-and-tender combination.

Marley's rise to international stardom did not diminish his loyalty to those left behind. As Chris Blackwell puts it, "Bob never separated himself from the people." He was always known as a "'umble yout'", an admirable trait he would never lose. If anything, his humility increased with his success. In the mid-Seventies, he drove a big, black BMW (as aforementioned, only because the letters stood for Bob Marley and The Wailers), but later in the decade ditched it in favour of a jeep, "an *old* jeep" he would stress. "I drive an old jeep so no one will say I'm drivin' a 'Bee Em Dubya' again. I cyaan stan' dat 'Bee Em Dubya'… pure trouble."

Junior Tucker remembers those times well. "Everybody knew he was a star, but he really was humble. He would always wear old jeans and a regular shirt, and drive up and down the road in a beat-up old jeep. Sometimes, he wouldn't even wear shoes… he looked like George the gardener." But, Tucker adds, even without the trappings, he could still rule the roost with few words. "They didn't call him 'The Skipper' for nothing."

Marley also stayed accessible. "There were no body-guards, no crew like people have today… he would talk to anyone," Tucker recalls, "and there was no office to go through… Bob would just hang out in the yard (at Hope Road), eat a food, write a song, an' play a little football." Ironically, say close friends, everyone around Marley was "tripping", while he never fell victim to his hype. Nor did his feet leave the ground: "Most people when they get money get withdrawn and foolish," he said. "Money is not my richness. My richness is to live and walk on the earth barefoot."

As the voice of Trench Town (and its "brother" communities), Marley's ghetto cred remained intact until he died. At the same time, his words touched enough of the disenchanted middle (and even upper) class, if not of Jamaica, of the world, that his music reached an astonishing number and range of people. His audiences never had

boundaries. Most of all, however, his message was for his people, and his words were meant to bring dignity to the ghetto.

"They say can anything good come out of Trench Town?" he sang plaintively, his presence alone answering the question in the affirmative.

Today, the people of Trench Town have no Bob, and are still fighting daily for survival. Still "in chains" as Marley said, and in 1999 worse off than ever before (the hard drugs that have brought a level of material prosperity to some people in these inner-city communities have also brought more guns, more crime, more deaths and less hope).

Marley's movement to "free the people with music" had a chance to do just that, but it was stopped—quite suddenly, and in mid-song, somewhere between the bridge and the chorus.

I KNOW

Recorded as part of the *Rastaman Vibration* sessions, 'I Know' was rejected for that album because Marley was unhappy with the mix. As he once asked an interviewer, "You know how plenty music get lost?", answering, "In the mix." Then, several years later, Family Man Barrett got a call from "bredda Bob" while Marley was a patient at Issels' clinic in Bavaria. Marley instructed Family Man to re-mix the tune and release it in Jamaica as a 12-inch "disco single". Family Man complied and 'I Know' had a good run on radio and in the clubs in both Jamaica and the UK.

One of the most emotional and affecting examples of his work on *Confrontation*—even non-believers are persuaded, if only momentarily, that Jah will indeed be there—'I Know' speaks to the downtrodden not just of Jamaica, but of any oppressed state. The words of the song "big up" Natty as guide on the way, and Jah as saviour, when you reach the finish line of the race.

It is telling that Marley thought of releasing this song while fighting the hardest battle of his life. Perhaps already sensing that he would lose, he was reassuring himself, as well as his worried fans, that Jah would be waiting for him, and that there was nothing at all to fear.

BLACKMAN REDEMPTION

Who better than a man of mixed blood to unify races? But as good as he was at treading the fine line between black and white, and understanding issues from both sides, the black side of his identity was by far the most developed. He was raised among blacks by a black woman. And he married one (though his affairs covered every color). Marley was also a champion of black causes as all his writing and interviews attest. 'Blackman Redemption' was written by Marley in the aftermath of the Hope Road shooting when his lyrics became more and more introspective.

Many before and after the reggae bard have prophesied a violent redemption. Marley saw redemption coming with acute clarity, but in his vision it came in peace. "Cool runnings", Marley "a beg" the people, and the phrase continued as a popular form of greeting in the early, and still irie, Eighties. The nation's mood had mellowed following the frightening election violence of 1980, Marley's death in 1981, and the adjustment to a new prime minister (the JLP's Edward Seaga). It was a good time in Jamaica, a time of new beginnings, and, ever so briefly, tangible hope. Marley's legacy of peace and love was still exerting a powerful influence on the land, and Rastafari lived. Soon would come the US-ordered "eradication of marijuana" drive (the trade-off for the IMF), and the subtle and apparently US-sanctioned switch from ganja trading to cocaine trafficking.

Cocaine first came into the island in a trickle. No one noticed it at first, but because the majority of Jamaicans didn't even knew what cocaine was, the trickle had become a flood. The island was suddenly faced with a new and deadly reality that was no longer confined to the ghetto.

And the deadly flood was not confined to coke. As the borders of Jamaica became cocaine-friendly, they also welcomed guns, state-of-the-art weapons that were smuggled, or paid through customs via a "let off", in every type of container. As imaginative as the ganja exporters had been in getting their product out of the country, so were their Colombian counterparts adept at getting their product, and by-product, in. The spirit of Rastafari, already weakened with the loss of its figurehead, was, like a lamb being willingly led to slaughter, almost eradicated along with the ganja.

Coke swept through the Rasta community like the plague, leaving devastation in its wake. Musicians were particularly affected, and so, in turn, was reggae music.

'Blackman Redemption' (presumably women didn't need redeeming) was recorded in 1978 as an optional track for *Survival*. Finally released in 1983, Jamaica's deliverance was about to be halted yet again.

MIX UP MIX UP

A missed single if ever there was one, 'Mix Up Mix Up', a tune of brilliant composition that has the power to lift the most subdued spirit and bring sunshine into the saddest of days, was culled from a 25-minute jam of Bob with his guitar and rhythm box, which Rita Marley came across on a two-track tape after her husband's death. Eight minutes were initially chosen from the jam. This was then edited down by Errol Browne to a standard mix of $3^3/_4$ minutes.

The improvised lyrics of 'Mix Up Mix Up' betray the unfinished state of the song, but the magical melody is strong enough to camoflage the fact that not all the words make sense.

Don Taylor says that The Skipper never wrote his words down, that they were all memorized and never committed to paper. Others remember his art director, Neville Garrick, writing down the words as Bob ad-libbed in the studio. But, some of Marley's songs did start off as written lyrics which, in common with most other songwriters, would be jotted down on any handy surface. Errol Browne confirms, however, that Jamaica's master tunesmith would generally compose both words and music simultaneously.

STIFF NECKED FOOLS

More formal than the British, and definitely more snobbish, those who ruled Jamaica following independence, were not, generally speaking, a tolerant set of people. Stiff-necked, uptight, inflexible, "lovers of vanity" (material possessions), are all words that have been used to describe the Jamaican establishment in the Sixties and Seventies, and represent the antithesis of Rasta ideology. Whether they were fools or not is open to interpretation. To Marley, they were, and he says in the song, "fools die for want of wisdom".

Michael Manley tried to diminish the post-colonial stiffness that lingered after the colonials left, by replacing jacket and tie (truly an absurdity in tropical climates) with the short-sleeved, cotton kareeba, which became his trademark attire and, during his tenure in office (but not any longer, since the current PNP prime minister favors suit and tie), acceptable dress for all events.

The concept for 'Stiff Necked Fools' harked back to The Wailers' early days and was taken from an old, unreleased song, then updated.

> ## "Fools die for want of wisdom"
> ### – Bob Marley

BUFFALO SOLDIER

The shared writing credit (with N G Williams aka King Sporty) acknowledges a large contribution to the song by Marley's old sparring partner from Studio One days. Family Man Barrett says that The Wailers collectively had the idea for the song and came up with part of it. King Sporty, another artist from the Coxsone Dodd stable, completed it and recorded it in demo form. "He brought the demo to Miami," says Barrett. "It was in a hip hop kinda version at first and we couldn't work with it, so we rearranged it." The resulting reggae rendition was an instant hit when the vinyl 45 finally hit the street in Jamaica in the early Eighties, putting the reggae don and his band back on local radio.

The story that 'Buffalo Soldier' tells is of four black regiments in the US army who, after the Civil War, waged a 25-year battle with six Indian tribes before the Indians (who suffered heavy casualties) were defeated. Fourteen of the black infantrymen—known as the "buffalo soldiers" by their Indian foes—were given the US Medal of Honour.

The song draws a parallel between the Buffalo Soldier and the Dreadlocks Rasta—both having been "stolen from Africa" and brought to a foreign land where they have had to fight for survival—and suggests that Marley himself is the keeper of the buffalo soldier flame this century.

THE ESCAPED SLAVE IN THE UNION ARMY.—[See Page 422.]

AN ESCAPED
SLAVE SOLDIER

THE LEGACY

Jah Live

Iron Lion Zion

Why Should I

Freedom Time

Roots

Comma Comma

Walk The Proud Land

Am A Do

Do You Feel The Same
Way Too

THE LEGACY OF BOB MARLEY

THE SPIRIT OF
BOB MARLEY
LIVES ON IN 1999

If nothing else, the early, tragic death of a revered musician guarantees immortality and, like Jimi Hendrix, Elvis Presley, and John Lennon before him, Marley's fan base, and sales continue to grow in his absence. Since his death in 1981, sales of the Marley catalog have, in the words of Chris Blackwell, "provided a constant revenue stream". The best seller of the posthumous releases is *Legend*, a compilation of some of the best of Marley's music, which has maintained a constant presence on the *Billboard Top Pop Catalog* chart, and which spent a record-breaking 19 weeks at Number One.

By choice, and in keeping with the Rastafarian refusal to acknowledge death, Bob Marley died intestate. Several people, including lawyer Dianne Jobson and doctor Pee Wee Herman, tried to persuade the dying Wailer to make a Will while he was still in Bavaria at the Issels Clinic, but the more they tried to persuade him to do so, the more the stubborn singer resisted their attempts.

"Nesta was a Rasta who believed in Universal rights and justice. And a Will is material not spiritual," says Mrs Booker. By not directing the disposition of his multi-million dollar "material" estate, Marley precipitated an acrimonious and controversial ten-year battle for the spoils. As his mother put it, "His body wasn't even cold in his tomb before the scavengers began fighting over his worldly goods."

In the beginning, Rita Marley and Jamaica's Mutual Security Bank were appointed co-executors. Marley's widow was later dismissed, however, for forging her late husband's name on numerous documents to transfer ownership to herself. Both she and her US attorneys, Zolt and Steinberg, were then sued for withholding funds totalling US $14 million—this being over and above the funds purportedly paid over by Don Taylor who claims, "everything that was still in my name I signed over to Rita".

Other disputes included a lawsuit brought against Mutual Security Bank by three of the 11 infant beneficiaries; a lawsuit against the estate initiated by the Wailers band; the near-eviction of Mother Booker from her estate-owned Miami home; and, a lawsuit against Booker for the recovery of US $500,000.

Cedella Booker talks of the first meeting of family and business associates after her son's death, and relates how shocked she was when she learned that she was not one of the 12 legal beneficiaries—widow Rita and Bob's nine natural or two adopted offspring. "The mother's portion," relates Booker, "was a puff of breeze… nothing", adding that she walked out of the meeting "disgusted".

It wasn't until 1991 that the sale of the assets of the estate of Robert Nesta Marley (estimated in 1981 to be worth US $30 million) would be resolved in favour of Chris Blackwell's company, Island Logic—interestingly, not a part of Island Records—for a sale price of US $12.5 million. For that amount, Blackwell, with the approval of all the heirs, purchased Marley's song catalog, recording royalties, distribution rights and Jamaican real estate, including 56 Hope Road and the Tuff Gong Studio and manufacturing complex on Marcus Garvey Drive. The Blackwell bid was successful (beating out a better offer from MCA for US $15.2 million, and besting his own first offer—approved by the executor but rejected by the UK Privy Council on appeal—of US $8.5 million in 1989) because his main interest, he said, was in making sure that the estate stayed in the family. "I don't want to own it," he said at the time, "I want only to manage the assets. I think I'm the best person for the job." Terms of the deal included the setting up of a Bob Marley Foundation which Blackwell was to manage for a period of ten years after which ownership would revert back to the widow and six of the children—the other five young heirs having settled for a cash payment of US $1 million each. After speculating that his investment would be paid back by the time ten years had elapsed, Blackwell then added: "I just wanted to be a part of something I helped to build up and I didn't want it to disappear in legal fees."

On the day the estate's destiny was finally decided, one newspaper reported that Rastafarian drummers sat outside the Supreme Court of Jamaica on Tower Street beating out the triumphant news that the life's work of the island's most celebrated Rastaman would stay in Jamaica. On that same day, in an uptown hospital, a baby was born to Bob's eldest son, Ziggy. The child was called Justice.

But none of the legal wrangling had stopped the music from playing, nor the royalties from pouring in.

> **"Nesta's body wasn't even cold in his tomb before the scavengers began fighting over his worldly goods"**
>
> **– Cedella Booker, Marley's mother**

(Nash), Arthur (Jenkins) and Danny (Sims)—tracks with disco overdubs, that Chris Blackwell called appalling.

In 1991, Island released *Talkin' Blues*, an album of mostly well-known songs, seven of which were recorded live by The Wailers in a closed session at the Record Plant in Sausalito, California, for an in-studio broadcast from San Francisco radio station KSAN in 1973. At this session, Peter Tosh was still very much present and Joe Higgs was standing in for a missing Bunny Wailer. The Wailers had just been bumped—after the first four dates—from a Sly & The Family Stone tour of the US. Added to the KSAN tracks, which (in addition to the familiar 'Rastaman Chant' and 'Get Up Stand Up') features lesser known works like 'You Can't Blame The Youth' and 'Walk The Proud Land', are alternate versions of two of the *Natty Dread* tunes, 'Talkin' Blues' and 'Ben' Down Low'. On the latter, Bob Marley plays flute, a feat which he played down, saying, laughingly, "Me nah really play the flute still, me jus' do dem lickle ting now an' den."

Also from the *Natty Dread* sessions came the previously unreleased 'Am A Do', described in the liner notes as "a session outtake", an unfinished "work in progress" that merited public exposure. Interspersed with the music are excerpts of an interview Marley did in 1975 during which he is asked what caused the dissolution of The Wailers. Indirectly calling Peter Tosh a hypocrite for not being honest with him (unlike Bunny Wailer who he says told him point-blank that he didn't want to tour), he concludes his answer by saying "up to now, me don' know wha' really 'appen".

In 1992, Island announced the release of *Songs Of Freedom*, a boxed set of four CDs that contained 77 songs. The collection started with the first song Marley recorded ('Judge Not' for Leslie Kong) and ended with a live version of 'Redemption Song' taken from The Skipper's last concert—Pittsburgh, September 23, 1980. Several of the *Songs Of Freedom* recordings are alternate mixes or live versions of studio songs. Two of the tracks—'Why Should I' and 'High Tide or Low Tide', had never been released in any form before. Originally issued in a limited-edition run of one million copies, which sold out quickly, demand for this set proved too alluring for label executives to ignore and, later in the decade, *Songs Of Freedom* was again made available.

Natural Mystic, 15 songs compiled by Chris Blackwell and Island Records' Trevor Wyatt, intended to

Rita Marley, during a telephone interview in 1990, was, as she talked, opening a royalty statement. An obviously pleased Rita said: "I never stop being surprised when I see how much money Bob's music makes… sometimes I say 'Wow,' when I see them [royalty statements]."

New releases also continued. After Island's 1983 release of *Confrontation* and *Legend* in 1984 came 1986's *Rebel Music*, which was just that, a compilation of the music that most represented the rebel, the rude bwoy from Second Street in Trench Town, whose revolutionary message touched the world. In 1988, Danny Sims released an album called, simply, *Bob Marley*, a tasteless attempt to update some early JAD—standing for Johnny

highlight the Rasta "messenjah", came out in 1995, along with a 14-page booklet that was illustrated with some of the best photographs ever taken of the singer—the Adrian Boot images of a radiant and visibly relaxed Robert Marley caught in a casual photo session at London's Keskidee Centre (for black arts) during the video shoot for 'Is This Love?'. The evocative shot that adorns *Legend* was also pulled from this cache.

Interestingly, the video produced that day was held back by his label for several years because they feared that a happy Bob cavorting with neighbourhood children would conflict with his militant image. The photographs surfaced when a cover shot for *Legend* was being sought and it was noticed that not only were they great shots, but that clearly visible on the Rastaman's finger is the "holy" ring that was once worn by Haile Selassie (given to Bob by the Emperor's son), and which, after some "inner circle" argument, was buried with him.

Difficult as it is to redefine an artist's existing work in a manner that is both tasteful and credible, Blackwell did it, and did it well, on 1997's *Dreams Of Freedom*, an album he conceptualised and Bill Laswell executed. This CD, called "an ambient translation of Bob Marley in dub" on popular cuts like 'So Much Trouble In The World 'and 'One Love', credits Laswell as "remix producer", with creative direction kudos given to Chris Blackwell.

Dub, the art of stripping a song down to its barest bones (drum and bass) and then dropping in instruments as the vibe dictates, is an integral part of reggae music. Blackwell has always loved dub and although he humbly accepts credit for the "dubbish-type things" on *Catch A Fire*, *Burnin'*, and *Natty Dread* ("because how Bob recorded was to not leave any space anywhere so that the voice and the backing voices and the horns and the keyboards were all filled… what I did was just bring them in here and there, and just give it much more air"), he says that he views that "more as arrangement". Distinguishing this from dub proper, the man who (after selling his company to Polgram for $350 million and staying within that constricting coporate structure for a while) has left Island Records behind and started a new company called Palm Pictures says that "I love the dub culture, but I don't understand it… I can't mix dub like Sly and Robbie or Family Man." *Dreams Of Freedom* is a testament to Blackwell's respect for dub culture, and for Marley and the extraordinary music he left behind.

The most recent Bob Marley And The Wailers release comes not from Island Records but from JAD. Titled *The Complete Bob Marley And The Wailers, 1967 To 1972 Part 1*, the three-CD set released in 1998 is the first of four, which, in total, will contain 200 songs recorded by Marley, Tosh and Wailer over the five-year period before Chris Blackwell came into the picture. Assembled by three Marley archivists—Roger Stefens, Bruno Blum and Jeremy Collingwood, the tracks in this extensive set include 23 previously unheard songs, some of which had to be digitally transferred from vinyl 45s because the masters were missing.

Oddly, if not predictably, this well-researched and documented collection has received little (read no) recognition in the land of Marley's birth, where a self-indulgent preoccupation with the computerised rhythms of dancehall has all but obliterated reggae's powerful call and world response.

Bob Marley lives on in the Jamaica of 1999, but the impact of his legacy on the rest of the world is not generally recognised by a "massive" that tends to see all of its entertainers as having equal global impact. The Bob Marley statue that stands by the National Arena is like the rest of Jamaica these days, unkempt and sullied by the litter of a lazy nation.

Now, 56 Hope Road, hidden behind the high concrete wall erected by Rita in the mid-Eighties, has been transformed from Marley's yard to Bob Marley's Museum, replete with restaurant, souvenir shop, a theatre and, says one of The Wailers with disgust, Bob's I'Scream.

The Marley family sets itself apart, and its members—more frequently spotted at the airport than on Kingston's streets where other reggae luminaries are regularly spotted—aren't seen to mingle with the rest of the reggae industry. Says one famous musician who was very close to Bob, "It come like dem feel superior".

To the steady stream of pilgrims who trek there in search of the Rasta dream of peace, love and unity, none of this matters. Whether cooling out in the serene countryside of Nine Miles or absorbing the tense, crackling air of a city often under violent siege, the

> ## "How Bob recorded was not to leave any space anywhere"
> **– Chris Blackwell**

faithful only want to come and touch the magic that was Bob Marley.

And some do.

"The beauty of Bob Marley," says Judy Mowatt, "is that so many years after his death, he's still bringing people together."

When Robert Nesta Marley died, he was in the midst of building a magnificent studio high on a hill in St Mary, close to the quiet town of Port Maria, and just a few miles down the coast from Chris Blackwell's GoldenEye estate in Oracabessa.

That unfinished work in progress (since sold by the Marleys), with its 15-foot high windows that look out to the ever-changing beauty of the Caribbean Sea, is a symbolic reminder of a life that as many see it, was tragically cut short.

The spirit of Rastafari would disagree that the Skipper had been short-changed, and argue that Marley "passed" at the right time, when the cornerstone of his life's work had already been firmly laid in concrete.

JAH LIVE

"We have a song called 'Jah Live'. Dem on de news say that our God is dead. But y'know, dem don' unerstan'."

Officially, Haile Selassie I, who was crowned Emperor of Ethiopia in 1930, died in Addis Ababa in 1975, but Rastas, who are nothing if not life-affirming (refusing to eat meat because it is "dedders"), never believed that their God had come to such a mortal end.

The pointed content of the lyrics lends credence to the probability that it was written around the time of Selassie's reported death as a celebration of the monarch's eternal life, but there are those who say it was written and recorded at Harry J's during the *Catch A Fire* sessions. If it was composed then it could be interpreted as prophetic.

It was also in the mid-Seventies that *Time* magazine brazenly announced on its cover that "God is Dead", a timely coincidence that extended the relevance of 'Jah Live' beyond Rasta to the Christian faiths of North America. "Yu cyaan kill God," said his servant, Bob, with more conviction than many in North America were feeling at a time when it was unfashionable to be spiritual.

'Jah Live' is on the *Songs Of Freedom* boxed set.

IRON LION ZION

'Iron Lion Zion', unfinished at the time of Bob's death, was completed with some tasteful overdubs and released by Island Records on *Confrontation*. It is a song of few words but strong emotion. When Marley sings "I am on the rock" (in Jamaica), and then he goes on to say he has to run like a fugitive, it is plain that of all the lyrics that allude to the Hope Road shooting, 'Iron Lion Zion' is the one that most directly addresses the residual pain Marley felt at being betrayed by his own countrymen in such a brutal way.

The bullet that remained in his arm until he died (leading his mother to ask if that could have caused the cancer) was not the only thing left behind by his attackers. His words give insight into what these days would be called post-traumatic stress disorder.

So intense must the after-effects of the shooting have been, that it is likely that Marley never really recovered from them.

But this song also convincingly reinforces Marley as a fighter. His response to the attempt to kill him is to summon his own strength, to be "iron like a lion" and conquer his fear and lingering paranoia.

NEW MUSICAL EXPRESS

NME

Setting standards: Jam album reviewed
P.39

JAMAICAN LION INNA CONCRETE JUNGLE

Bob Marley in Harlem
By NEIL SPENCER

MARLEY THE FIGHTER:
HE SUMMONED HIS
STRENGTH TO BE
'IRON LIKE A LION'

WHY SHOULD I

Rastafari gave hope to the ghetto; hope in a place where life for many begins and ends on a hot and dusty dead-end street, but where a bare-foot boy named Robert Nesta Marley found a way out. Marley's belief was that if he could do it, so could others—the fact that he had immense talent being secondary, he held, to the power of self-worth.

But self-worth is as rare as extraordinary talent in a place where each daybreak comes not with the promise of a new day but with the pain of yesterday, and the nights are filled not with the joy and laughter that echoes down the hills from the terraces of upper St Andrew, but with the unrelenting "barking" of guns, a sound so commonplace in the ghetto that people are no longer awakened by the sound.

Marley's unfinished mission was to change the mindset of the poor and downtrodden, and lead his people to a better place.

Originally recorded in 1971, and found in Rita Marley's vault of Marley material after his death, 'Why Should I' was produced by the Wailers, with additional rhythm production by Errol Browne.

FREEDOM TIME

Officially, Jamaica and its people were free when this song was written in the early Sixties, after the island's independence from Britain. But then, as now, "freedom" is relative and, to the prisoner of the ghetto, freedom is as far (if not further) away today as it was during slavery. Chains of the mind or the body confine with equal strength.

The Rastas were the first to popularize the concept of mental slavery, and Bob Marley the first to sing of it (in 'Redemption Song').

Still, recognition of its existence doesn't equal change. The conditions which imprisoned ghetto minds in Marley's time are still very much intact, and too valuable a tool of Jamaica's post-Colonial rulers to expect change any time soon.

With the proclamation of freedom, "the slave(s) to this country" may have left the plantation, but the master/slave tradition merely took on another form. Freedom Time is still a'comin'.

Marley had a habit of pulling phrases from existing lyrics and inserting them into another song. He also did this with melody lines. From 'Freedom Time' he took the line "didn't I build the cabin, didn't I plant the corn" and planted it in 'Crazy Baldhead'.

'Freedom Time' is significant for being the first song released on the Wailers Wail 'N Soul 'M label.

ROOTS

Roots are to Rastafari what the umbilical cord is to the unborn child—its life source. Some are leaves and some are branches, Marley reminds, "but I'n'I are the roots", meaning that Rastafari and roots are one with the Creator. A Rastaman is a rootsman and vice versa. Because of this, he continues, "nothing that dividers can do can separate us from our father."

Though Rastas preach against living in the past—"forward evah, backwards nevah" being a favourite expression—the roots of Rastafari that burrow deep into the soul of Africa are the wellspring from which everything comes. This—the past merging with the present and the future—must not only be acknowledged, it is believed, but embraced.

The future direction of the Rastafarian movement was seriously hindered by the premature loss of Bob Marley. While never officially declared its leader, he was nonetheless a unifying presence. He was also a figure-head who could be followed, a suitable companion to "trod to creation" with.

The collective energy that he amassed dissipated when he left, curtailing Rasta's considerable power and blurring its once clear and purposeful path.

COMMA COMMA

One of seven songs sequenced together as an acoustic demo by Marley, and released on the *Songs Of Freedom* set, 'Comma Comma' was recorded, along with the other six tracks by keyboardist Rabbit Bundrick in Bob's bedroom in Stockholm in the summer of 1971. Marley was in Sweden to work on songs for a film soundtrack with Johnny Nash, for whom the demo was cut.

Neither the film nor the soundtrack ever went anywhere, but Nash later covered two of the tunes on the medley.

The first, 'Stir It Up, was the song that gave Bob Marley his first international hit as a songwriter. The second, 'Comma Comma', while not as big a hit as 'Stir It Up', also did well.

Marley was not a great guitarist (and "never tuned his Bundrick", says Bundrick) but played well enough to accompany himself on acoustic renditions of his work. His interest in the instrument was apparent from early on and his first home-made guitar was fashioned by an uncle out of goatskin and bamboo.

The lyric of 'Comma Comma' is simplistic (read trite) and likely one of Marley's first attempts at song-writing. It is also typical of the light R&B fare recorded for JAD Records.

> "The beauty of Bob Marley is that so many years after his death, he's still bringing people together"
>
> **– Judy Mowatt**

WALK THE PROUD LAND

Originally recorded as 'Rude Boy' in the ska era of the Sixties, 'Walk The Proud Land' is another example of how Marley recycled both whole songs and snippets of either lyrics or melodies. He did this throughout his career for both artistic and materialistic reasons.

'Walk The Proud Land' is a verbal nod to the two cultures which shaped Robert Nesta Marley—the English Colonialists who had just left and the Afrocentric Rastafarians who were just coming into their own. The invitation in the song to 'Skank Quadrille' combines the loose-limbed and free movements of the Rasta skank with the formal British dancing patterns of the Quadrille.

Before Jamaica became independent—after 300

years of British rule and a few earlier years under Spanish domination—the island's social manners and mores were distinctly English, and although the African heritage of the slaves was preserved among themselves, it was only after Independence that its influence was felt in any formative way. But, as afternoon tea and military bands receded into the Colonial past, and ackee and saltfish and reggae bands emerged as the island's future, for a brief and beautiful time, the best of both worlds made Jamaica a magical place to be.

AM A DO

Described as "an unfinished work in progress" in the liner notes, and released only because of what Island Records felt was its "inherent quality", 'Am A Do' is a love song with a suggestive undertone, something that its writer was very good at pulling off. Unlike the crass, coarse and vulgar expressions that ride today's rhythms of dancehall, the music of Bob Marley always suggested rather than graphically described sexual intimacy, thereby communicating much stronger feelings of sensuality.

Emotionally distant much of the time, Bob let his music do the dangerous work. At once intimate and impersonal, he was able to express the most personal of feelings in a safe way. 'Am A Do', recorded in 1974, tells her how it is, but from a comfortable distance.

The female harmony of the I'Threes on this track contrasts with the seven live recordings that make up the bulk of *Talkin' Blues* and marks the transition from one Wailers incarnation to the next.

THE I'THREES
HAD A UNIQUE
BLEND OF HARMONIES

DO YOU FEEL THE SAME WAY TOO

This innocent love song, written when Marley was a Trench Town teenager, was released as part of the *Destiny* album in 1999. Significant for having been recorded—on July 8, 1965—in the same Studio One session as 'One Love', and that session being notable as the first to utilise Coxsone Dodd's Ampex 252 two-track machine (purchased from Ken Khouri), 'Do You Feel The Same Way Too' is backed by members of the famed Skatalites (who played on many of Dodd's early tunes) and features a solo by alto saxophonist Lester Sterling.

The early sessions at 13 Brentford Road were marked by the teamwork of the many talents that gathered there. Roland Alphonso, another saxophonist, is the man Dodd credits with teaching The Wailers "the beats per bar, to check to know where to come in and where to stop singing".

Keyboardist Jackie Mittoo (another musician associated

many of the city's youths, a commitment to Rastafarianism. In October, Bob Marley returns to Jamaica and he, too, hears the call of Rastafari. He also heeds his instinct to "control my own destiny" and with his two partners, and whatever cash he has managed to save from his factory job, starts The Wailers own record label—Wail'N Soul'M. The first single released on Wail'N Soul'M is 'Freedom Time', backed by 'Bend Down Low'. Other songs that mark this year include the sexy 'Stir It Up' and party favourite 'Nice Time'.

1967
The Wailers' first shop (Wail'N Soul'M) is opened at 18a Greenwich Road, the home of Rita Marley where the newlyweds first live. Distribution to other local retail outlets is done by bicycle or on foot by the three Wailers, and by Rita Marley who, so the story goes, carries them on her head. Bunny Wailer is put in jail for 15 months on a trumped-up ganja charge, but this doesn't stop the musical momentum of the still-struggling group.
The financial situation is eased later in the year when the group meets up with American singer Johnny Nash and producer Danny Sims, who sign the trio to their company, JAD Records, giving each of The Wailers a $50.00 a week retainer. Marley and Tosh also sign songwriting contracts with Sims' publishing company, Cayman Music. Songs like 'Stepping Razor', 'Don't Rock My Boat' and 'Soul Rebel' are recorded for Sims, Nash and third partner Arthur Jenkins. The relationship with JAD would last until 1972 and result in the recording of more than 80 songs.

1968
Reggae, (a new music characterised by the downbeat being on 2 and 4 instead of 1 and 3 common to other music of 4/4 time) is born, and formalised by Toots And The Maytals' single, 'Do The Reggay'.

1969
Bob Marley makes his second trip to the United States with wife Rita.

1970
The Wailers record numerous singles for Leslie Kong who, without permission, then releases an album titled *The Best Of The Wailers*. Kong dies shortly after releasing this album of a heart attack while still in his thirties. Producer Lee "Scratch" Perry, who has known The Wailers since his engineering and selector days with Coxsone Dodd, then begins to produce the talented trio, teaming them up with his backing band, The Upsetters, and starts what would be a lifelong musical affiliation for Bob with the bass and drum-playing Barrett brothers, Family Man and Carly. 'Kaya', 'African Herbsman' and '400 Years' are some of the tracks recorded with Perry, who would later be credited as having produced the real "best of The Wailers". But Perry also infuriates The Wailers by releasing three albums internationally through Trojan Records in England.

1972
Disillusioned with Nash, Sims and CBS (which fails to promote *Reggae On Broadway*) The Wailers go to see Chris Blackwell who signs them to Island, gives them £4,000 and sends them back to Jamaica to record an album, which, contrary to the Jamaican music industry norm of taking the money and not delivering, is ready to mix in a matter of weeks. Blackwell hears the album and is "completely knocked out" by how "fantastic, how progressive" the music is. Michael Manley is elected as Prime Minister of Jamaica on a socialist ticket.

1973
The Wailers form Tough Gang, a company whose name is soon modified to "Tuff Gong", said to be one of Marley's nicknames. The Wailers are now producing much of their work themselves and record 'Concrete Jungle', 'Trenchtown Rock' and 'Guava Jelly'. The Wailers go to London for JAD Records where they record Reggae On Broadway for CBS. Marley then accompanies Johnny Nash to Sweden to write songs for a B-movie soundtrack.

1973
Catch A Fire is released, uniquely packaged in a "Zippo lighter sleeve", and attracts critical raves from the fickle British press. The group's first tour of Europe takes place during the summer of 1973. On the promotional tour of the US, The Wailers share billing with Bruce Springsteen at New York's Max's Kansas City. Later in the year, The Wailers return to Kingston to record what would become *Burnin'*, their second album for Island and their last as The Wailers.

1973
Burnin' is released to the same kind of critical acclaim that was accorded *Catch A Fire*. European and US tours are arranged, but during the UK leg, Peter Tosh drops out of the group. Joe Higgs subs for the missing member in the US, but by the time that is over, Bunny Wailer has also left. Bob Marley, now a solo act, teams up with the Barrett brothers (who have been touring with The Wailers since *Catch A Fire*) and becomes Bob Marley And The Wailers.
Natty Dread is recorded later in 1974, and the I'Threes —a female trio consisting of Rita Marley, Marcia Griffiths and Judy Mowatt—is brought in to provide backing vocals for the 1975 tour. In 1974, Marley moves from Trench Town to Island House at 56 Hope Road (a property he would buy from Blackwell a couple of years later), and Don Taylor enters Marley's life, and would go on to serve as his manager for several years.

1974

Island releases *Natty Dread* and the transition from group to solo act goes well, Marley being hailed as a musical Messiah. Live shows at venues like London's Lyceum corroborate Marley's extraordinary talent. In the US, a show at LA's Roxy draws an audience that includes Bob Dylan, Jack Nicholson, Ringo Starr and George Harrison. Marley's first live album, entitled *Live! Bob Marley And The Wailers*, taken from the Lyceum show, follows *Natty Dread* on the Island release schedule for 1974.

1975

Emperor Haile Selassie dies and Marley writes 'Jah Live', an affirmation of the Rasta belief that Selassie couldn't die. The Wailers perform a still-remembered set at London's Lyceum with Third World opening.

1976

Rastaman Vibration puts Marley and The Wailers into the US Top 10 for the first time. The world tour in support of this release is sold-out at most stops. On his return to Jamaica, Marley conceives the idea of a free concert to be called Smile Jamaica and gets the cooperation of Michael Manley who is running for re-election, with the proviso that the concert be apolitical. Manley, however, seizes the opportunity to cash in on Marley's popularity and, as soon as the concert's date (December 5) is announced, calls the election for a couple of weeks later. On December 3, gunmen break into 56 Hope Road, shooting Marley, wife Rita and manager Don Taylor. After much hesitation, a still-bandaged Marley performs at the Smile Jamaica concert following which he goes into exile—in the Bahamas and Britain—for 18 months.

1977

In London, Marley continues his affair with Cindy Breakespeare, recording, at Island's Basing Street studio, the songs for what would become *Exodus* and *Kaya,* released in 1977 and 1978 respectively. Embarking on the *Exodus* tour, The Wailers complete their itinerary in Europe, but cancel the US leg when Marley, who has reactivated an old toe injury playing soccer in Paris, is diagnosed with melanoma in his toe. On the advice of the Crown Prince of Ethiopia, Asfa Wasson (Selassie's son), Marley opts not to have the toe amputated as advised by a Harley Street physician, but to seek alternate treatment in Miami. He stays in Miami for five months during which he has part of his toe removed and is given a melanoma-free prognosis.

1978

Kaya is released to mixed reviews. Much is made of the fact that the romantic tone of the album is an indication that the hard-hitting Rastaman has gone "soft", a criticism he takes in his stride. On February 28, Marley returns to Jamaica for the first time since he was shot, and on April 22, Marley and The Wailers perform at the legendary One Love concert. In a now-famous climax to this show, Marley invites the incumbent Michael Manley and his arch-rival, the opposition leader, Edward Seaga, to join him onstage in a show of reconciliation. Holding both of their hands together above him, Marley triumphantly ad-libs to the background strains of 'Jamming', giving everyone the hope (short-lived as it turns out) of a united Jamaica. Several months after this show, Marley is awarded the United Nations Peace Medal in New York. His *Kaya* tour takes him into even bigger sold-out venues. *Babylon By Bus*, a second live album, is taken from this tour.

1979

This is the year of *Survival* and The Wailers first foray into the Far East. As well as Japan, they tour New Zealand and Australia.

1980

Island Records releases *Uprising*, and Bob Marley And The Wailers usher in the independence of Zimbabwe on April 17, with a rousing concert in Salisbury. Marley's highly emotional rendition of the song 'Zimbabwe', is marked by the fact that the entire audience knows the words. The European tour for *Uprising* follows, marked by an astounding concert in Milan which draws an estimated 100,000 people. The US tour starts in September with two sold-out shows opening for The Commodores at Madison Square Gardens. The night after the second show, Marley collapses while jogging in Central Park. Struggling to continue the tour, Marley decides to travel to Pittsburgh, the next stop on the schedule, for what would be his final concert. He returns to New York where doctors confirm that the melanoma has spread to other parts of his body, and tell him that it is terminal.

1981

Is a final attempt to save his life, Bob Marley goes to Bavaria in late 1980 to receive treatment at the clinic of Dr Josef Issels, a man with a reputation for some success in treating terminal cancer. This last hope is dashed in May of 1981 when Issels says he can do no more for the ailing singer. Leaving for Jamaica, Marley only makes it as far as Miami, where, on May 11, he dies at that city's Cedars of Lebanon hospital. A state funeral is held for Robert Nesta Marley OD (he was given Jamaica's highest honour, the Order of Distinction in February) on May 21 at Kingston's National Arena. Marley is buried where he was born, in Nine Miles atop a small hill where, as a child, he used to sit and dream.

DISCOGRAPHY

SINGLES

Title: Judge Not
Producer: Leslie Kong
Date: 1961

Title: I'm Still Waiting
Producer: Coxsone Dodd
Date: 1963

Title: Bend Down Low

Title: Simmer Down

Title: Bus' Dem Shut
Producer: Wailers
Date: 1966

Title Screw Face

Title: One Cup Of Coffee
Producer: Leslie Kong
Date: 1961

Title: Mellow Mood
Producer: Wailers
Date: 1971

Title: Duppy Conqueror
Producer: Leslie Kong
Date: 1969 (first of seven versions)

Title: Nice Time
Producer: Wailers
Date: 1967

Title: Cornerstone
Producer: Lee Scratch Perry
Date: 1969

Title: (I'm Gonna) Put it On
Producer: Coxsone Dodd
Date: 1963-1966

Title: Put It On
Producer: Lee Scratch Perry
Date: 1969

ALBUMS

1971
The Best Of The Wailers
Beverley's
Produced by Leslie Kong

Tracks:
Soul Shakedown Party, Stop The Train, Caution, Soul Captives, Go Tell It On The Mountain, Can't You See, Soon Come, Cheer Up, Back Out, Do It Twice

1973
Catch a Fire
Island Records
Produced by Chris Blackwell and Bob Marley

Tracks:
Concrete Jungle, Slave Driver, 400 Years, Stop That train, Baby We've Got A Date (Rock it Baby), Stir It Up, Kinky Reggae, No More Trouble, Midnight Ravers

1973
Burnin'
Island Records
Produced by Chris Blackwell and Bob Marley

Tracks:
Get Up Stand Up, Hallelujah Train, I Shot the Sheriff, Burnin' And Lootin', Put It On, Small Axe, Pass it On, Duppy Conqueror, One Foundation, Rastaman Chant

1974
Natty Dread
Island Records
Produced by Chris Blackwell and The Wailers

Tracks:
Lively Up Yourself, No Woman No Cry, Them Belly Full (But We Hungry), Rebel Music (3 o'clock Roadblock), So Jah Seh, Natty Dread, Bend Down Low, Talkin' Blues, Revolution

1974
The Best Of Bob Marley And The Wailers
Studio One
Produced by Coxsone Dodd
Tracks:
I am Going Home, Bend Down Low, Mr Talkative, Ruddie, Cry To Me, Wings Of A

Dove, Small Axe, Love Won't Be Mine, Dancing shoes, Sunday Morning, He Who Feels It Knows it, Straight And Narrow Way

1975
Soul Rebels
Bob Marley And The Wailers
Produced by Lee Perry

Tracks:
Try Me, It's Alright, No Sympathy, My Cup, Soul Almighty, Rebels Hop, Corner Stone, 400 Years, No Water, Reaction, My Sympathy.

1975
Live! Bob Marley And The Wailers
Island Records
Produced by Steve Smith and Chris Blackwell

Tracks:
Trenchtown Rock, Burnin' And Lootin', Them Belly Full, Lively Up Yourself, No Woman No Cry, I Shot The Sheriff, Get Up Stand Up.

1976
Soul Revolution
Bob Marley And The Wailers
Produced by Lee Perry

Tracks:
Keep On Moving, Don't Rock My Boat, Put It On, Fussing And Fighting, Duppy Conqueror, Memphis, Riding High, Kaya, African Herbsman, Stand Alone, Sun Is Shining.

1976
Rastaman Vibration
Island Records
Produced by Bob Marley And The Wailers

Tracks:
Positive Vibration, Roots, Rock, Reggae, Johnny Was, Cry To Me, Want More, Crazy Baldhead, Who The Cap Fit, Night Shift, War, Rat Race

1977
Exodus
Island Records
Produced by Bob Marley And The Wailers

Tracks:
Natural Mystic, So Much Things To Say, Guiltiness, The Heathen, Exodus, Jamming, Waiting in Vain, Turn Your Lights Down Low,

Three Little Birds, One Love/People Get Ready

1978
Kaya
Island Records
Produced by Bob Marley And The Wailers

Tracks:
Easy Skanking, Kaya, Sun Is Shining, Is This Love?, Satisfy My Soul, She's Gone, Misty Morning, Crisis, Running Away, Time Will Tell

1978
Babylon By Bus, Island Records, Produced by Bob Marley And The Wailers

Tracks:
Positive Vibration, Punky Reggae Party, Exodus, Stir It Up, Rat Race, Concrete Jungle, Kinky Reggae, Lively Up Yourself, Rebel Music, War, No More Trouble, Is This Love?, The Heathen, Jamming.

1979
Survival
Island Records
Produced by Bob Marley And The Wailers and Alex Sadkin

Tracks:
Up And Live, Africa Unite, One Drop, Ride Natty Ride, Ambush In The Night, So Much Trouble In The World, Zimbabwe, Top Rankin', Babylon System, Survival

1980
Uprising, Island Records
Produced by Bob Marley And The Wailers

Tracks:
Coming In From the Cold, Real Situation, Bad Card, We And Dem, Work, Zion Train, Pimper's Paradise, Could You Be Loved?, Forever Living Jah, Redemption Song

1983
Confrontation, Island Records
Produced by Chris Blackwell and Rita Marley

Tracks:
Mix Up Mix Up, Buffalo Soldiers, Come We Go Burn Down Babylon, I Know, Stiff Necked Fools, Jump Nyabinghi, Trench Town, Give Thanks And Praises, Blackman Redemption.

1984
Legend
Island Records

Tracks:
Is This Love?, No Woman No Cry, Could You Be Loved?, Three Little Birds, Buffalo Soldier, Get Up Stand Up, Stir It Up, One Love/People Get Ready, I Shot The Sheriff, Waiting In Vain, Redemption Song, Satisfy My Soul, Exodus, Jamming

1986
Rebel Music
Island Records

Tracks:
Music, So Much Trouble In The World, Them Belly Full (But We Hungry), Rat Race, War/No More Trouble, Roots, Slave Driver, Ride Natty Ride, Crazy Baldhead, Get Up Stand Up

1991
Talkin' Blues
Island Records

Tracks:
Talkin' Blues. Burnin' And Lootin', Kinky Reggae, Get Up Stand Up, Slave Driver, Walk The Proud Land, You Can't Blame The Youth, Rastaman Chant, Am-A-Do, Bend Down Low, I Shot The Sheriff

1992
Songs Of Freedom
Island Records

Tracks:
Judge Not, One Cup Of Coffee, Simmer Down, I'm Still Waiting, One Love/People Get Ready, Put It On, Bus' Dem Shut, Mellow Mood, Bend Down Low, Hypocrite, Stir It Up, Nice Time, Thank You Lord, Hammer, Caution, Back Out, Soul Shake Down Party, Do It Twice, Soul Rebel, Sun Is Shining, Don't Rock The Boat, Small Axe, Duppy Conqueror, Mr Brown, Screw Face, Lick Samba, Trenchtown Rock, Craven Choke Puppy, Guava Jelly, Acoustic Medley (a) Guava Jelly, (b) This Train, (c) Cornerstone, (d) Comma Comma, (e) Dewdrops, (f) Stir It Up, (g) I'm Hurtin' Inside, High Tide Or Low Tide, Slave Driver, No More Trouble, Concrete Jungle, Get Up Stand Up, Rastaman Chant, Burnin' And Lootin', Iron Lion Zion, Lively Up Yourself, Natty Dread, I Shot The Sheriff, No Woman No Cry, Who the Cap Fit, Jah Live, Crazy Baldhead, War, Johnny Was, Rat Race, Jamming, Waiting In Vain, Exodus, Natural Mystic, Three Little Birds, Running Away, Keep On Moving, Easy Skanking, Is This Love?, Smile Jamaica, Time Will Tell, Africa Unite, Survival, One Drop (Dub of One Drop), Zimbabwe, So Much Trouble In The World, Ride Natty Ride, Babylon System, Coming In From The Cold, Real Situation, Bad Card, Could You Be Loved?, Forever Loving Jah, Rastaman Live Up, Give Thanks And Praises, One Love/People Get Ready, Why Should I?, Redemption Song

1995
Natural Mystic
Island Records
Compiled by Chris Blackwell and Trevor Wyatt

Tracks:
Natural Mystic, Easy Skanking, Iron Lion Zion, Crazy Baldhead, So Much Trouble In The World, War, Africa Unite, Trenchtown Rock, Keep On Moving, Sun Is Shining, Who The Cap Fit, One Drop, Roots Rock Reggae, Pimper's Paradise, Time Will Tell.

1997
Dreams Of Freedom
Island Records
Re-Mix Production by Bill Laswell

Tracks:
Rebel Music (3 o'clock Roadblock), No Woman No Cry, The Heathen, Them Belly Full (But We Hungry), Waiting In Vain, So Much Trouble In The World, Exodus, Burnin' And Lootin', Is This Love?, One Love (People Get Ready), Midnight Ravers

1999
Destiny
Heartbeat Records
Produced by Clement "Sir Coxsone" Dodd

Tracks:
Destiny, Wages Of Love, Do You Feel The Same Way Too?, Your Love, Don't Ever Leave Me (Take One), Don't Ever Leave Me (Take 2), I Need You So, Rock Sweet Rock, Another Dance, I Stand Predominant, Where Is My Mother (acoustic version), Where Is My Mother (band take), Dance With Me, What's New Pussycat, Treat Me Good, Jerking Time aka Jerk In Time, Do It Right, Let the Love Be Seen In Me.

INDEX